Whiteline

Whiteline

A Collection of Short Stories

By

David Lee Knight

Published by DLK Publishing in 2017

First Printing: 2017

DLK Publishing

ISBN: 978-1-973-10403-2

For Anne

Thank you for the editing, proof reading and unending support.

"….twenty years of experience should not be confused with one year of experience repeated twenty times……"

CONTENTS

Bright Meadow

Her eyes sparkled, just a little; she knew he liked that.

His hand trembled slightly as his finger traced the line of her cheekbone and tucked an errant wisp of hair back behind her ear.

"Ah", he let out a breath, "you're so beautiful".

She laughed. "I'm your servant, sir, you chose me. Of course I'm beautiful."

"Hmmmph."

She smiled, looked away.

They were on the deck overlooking the garden, sitting in padded wooden loungers, where for the last several months he had spent a good part of the day. She had come out to join him after finishing up in the kitchen, bringing two glasses of wine with her. They often liked to spend the warmer evenings here, talking or reading and watching the night steal in.

A casual observer, who did not know her, would not have described her as beautiful, and although may have agreed she could pass for thirty-five, there was something in her eyes that would have made it more likely, if pressed, they would opt for older. She had a perfectly symmetrical, finely featured face with glossy black hair kept shoulder short which topped a very tall, athletic body. Her skin was olive coloured and she smelled like summer.

"House!"

Slight pause. "Yes, Sir." The house computer replied.

"Garden lights, please."

Immediately lights came on all over the garden, picking out the paths with rows of light, outlining the lawns, highlighting shrubs and trees and backlighting the pond.

He sighed. "House, have you been adding lights without me knowing?"

Long pause. "The mobiles have done some repairs and minor modifications, Sir, I hope you approve."

The mobiles were small drones with various attachments that the House used for physical jobs such as cleaning and vacuuming and minor repairs.

"Everything off but the trees, please."

The House acknowledged and most of the lights faded, leaving only the strategically placed spotlights that lit the trees from below which created a glowing green haze around the garden.

"This house is yours, you know that don't you and whatever else is left."

"Shush, you know I have never wanted anything from you, and besides William expects it to be his I'm sure."

"My nephew will get what he deserves, actually more than he deserves but hopefully the cash will keep him quiet.

She put her hand on his arm.

"Let's just enjoy the evening".

"I know it may not hold up legally and Billy will almost certainly challenge my will, but I need you to know this. I have left you this house; it's your home after all and half of everything else.

"Sir, I neither need nor want anything from you – you know that".

"Ok, enough." He sat back sipping at his wine and a companionable silence grew around them.

She still found these conversations unnerving although she had become more used to them. He had always been like this. When she had first come to work for him and was still struggling with the finer points of the English language she had had to seek advice from her mentor at the Centre several times a day. She had after all expected to be treated like a slave, or at best a lowly servant, certainly not an equal. She felt she should say something more appreciative but as she turned to look at him she saw his eyes were closed and his face was ashen.

"It's getting cold I think, time for bed." She got up, crouched beside him, squirmed one arm beneath his skinny thighs and the other behind his back. She straightened her knees and stood lifting his weight as if he was a baby.

"House?"

"Yes."

"We're going to bed. Lights please, bed to body temperature."

"Done, temperature estimated complete 90 seconds"

"Thank you, House."

She carried him into the bedroom. She laid him down gently, pulled the cover over his wasted frame, checked his pulse and pressure and attached the monitor sensors to his temple and chest.

After a few minutes his colour returned and he managed a weak smile.

"Chemo tonight?" he said gesturing at the machinery filling the space between bed and wall.

"Can't do any harm". She connected the tubes to him and started the medpump.

"Not much good either." He patted the bed beside him.

"Feeling better then are we," she smiled. She had always shared his bed, but it had been at least eighteen months since anything physical had occurred. She did not mind either way.

When she had finished setting the machine she climbed in beside him and let her head rest on his chest with just enough weight that he could feel it but not discomfort him. From here she could also monitor the machine.

His voice was a raspy whisper but the words were still clear.

"Not long now."

"No sir, a few days at most."

"I love you and I thank you for all you have done for me."

"Shush."

He slept.

The treatment, even if it could no longer hold back the advanced stages of the illness, at least assured him of a good night's sleep. She got up and disconnected the tubes so he could turn naturally. She looked down at his sleeping face less haggard now that he was sleeping but still showing the ravages of two years of lost battles.

She called up a memory of him when he had first come to the Centre. He was handsomely lived-in then. His wife had been dead for several years and he needed a housekeeper and companion. It was a perfect trade; she got a home and useful employment and he got a very hard working housekeeper.

He had taken her home and never asked about anything in her past and never in all their years together had he ever mentioned where she had come from. He had treated her with respect from the very first, and let her know that this was her home and she had a place here. She belonged here. In a strange way she had grown into that – she knew it would end soon.

He knew.

She sat with him holding his hand listening to each breath until, simply, the next breath never came.

She waited to see if any sudden rush of emotion would well up around her. None did.

Had he loved her? He had said the words to her precisely four times in their years together, the last only a few days ago. She could recall in perfect clarity the circumstances of each.

It confused her still; it went against everything she had been taught. But it had been more than that. He had treated her like someone he wanted to get to know, to teach, to learn from, and to share life with. The Centre had told her he was just eccentric and she had just been lucky and should go along with it. She was owned by him - he could do and say what he wanted.

Love. She had understood what it should be from the books and films that he had shared with her. The best were always those that touched him deeply. She knew those were the ones that brought the quiet tears to his eyes.

But what was in the stories did not fully explain the concept. The stories were often about the search, the hunt, the serendipity of it all. Why was it that often two people who hated each other at first sight finally figured out that they were soul mates two hours later? The stories were about the overcoming of denial, of external factors, or the actions of other people to keep the lovers apart but they often end at the beginning of love. To her it remained as confusing as ever.

She turned him onto his back. His face looked composed, restful and younger. She smoothed his thin hair down and placed his hands across his chest.

She wished she could cry for him, like in the books. She recalled a haiku type poem he had once quoted to her - the comfort in the warmth of a tear.

She went into the bathroom, wet her finger with hot water and deposited a tear like drop beneath one eye. She monitored its track and warmth in the mirror as it slowly trickled down her face. After a while she went back into the bedroom.

William came in without bothering to announce his arrival and the door let him in unchallenged. He was with a short tubby man wearing a fashionable shiny suit which was too big and too young for him.

"Mmm, well," the stranger ran his eyes over her, "I didn't know your uncle had an effing bot."

"Technically I'm not a robot, sir. Organic body, kevlar frame and electronic mind – android or artificial being, AB for short if you prefer, would be a more accurate description.

William waved her quiet.

"Oh, it's just a medical model. I've sold it on to a family in Edinburgh already. It's going next week."

William turned to her. This is Clifford, my lawyer. We'll be going through some of my uncle's papers today. You'll clean the house and tomorrow the furniture will be cleared into storage ready for the sale of the house. You stay here until I've been paid for you. There's a pickup for my uncle at 9 tomorrow. They'll take him to the crematorium - have him ready."

"Yes sir."

"Where is he?"

"In the bedroom. Do you wish to see him?"

"That won't be necessary. Bring coffee to the study".

"Yes sir."

The lawyer walked across the kitchen and stood up close to her. Too close. He looked her arrogantly up and down. He put his hands on her shoulders and turned her round. She kept the turn going so that she was again facing him and he was forced to drop his hands.

"Hmmm, not bad for a bot. Maybe I could borrow her for a few days before she gets sold?" He leered at William.

"It's a medical model, I told you. Let's get on with this," said William turning towards the door.

"Yes I'm a medical model, I have no sexual orifices." A green light started flashing in the upper right of her visual field and 'software conflict alert' in small text scrolled around beneath it.

William snorted in disgust and headed out the door.

Clifford smirked, "Well I can see one."

Suddenly, without thinking, she knelt in front of the lawyer extending all her muscle groups to the maximum. The indicator light in her visual field was flashing urgent amber even before her knees touched the floor. Her head was almost level with the lawyer's chest. She opened her mouth wide, again stretching every muscle to capacity and spoke without moving the lips of her very wide open mouth.

"Can you reach, sir? I'm not really suitable for this kind of work I'm afraid, sir, no sexual nuance software or physical control limits, and my jaw clamp maximum force is not safety restricted, sir. Do you wish me to recite the safety warning related to sexual interaction with a non-modified artificial being and the risks associated with it, sir?"

Clifford froze, his eyes widened, he stood for long seconds and eventually scurried after his client. Stuck his head back round the door a few moments later and said

"You're getting wiped, bitch".

The amber light was flashing wildly and 'software conflict – urgent attention required' scrolled continuously across her vision.

Had she actually threatened a human? Maybe, a veiled threat – did that count? But in any case she had definitely told her first lie. She started to make the coffee.

She was not just a medical model, nor a sex model. She was a servant/companion model with a full sexual upgrade and medical nurse upgrade. Poor Billy did not know how much she was actually worth.

When it became obvious that he required more of her than servant or companion, the Centre had offered an upgrade and several weeks of modifications had made her a woman. When she returned home he had treated her with great concern as if she had been ill in hospital which was not far from the truth. When he became ill, the Centre had again intervened and suggested the medical upgrade.

William and the lawyer left an hour or so later looking angry and clutching reams of paper. They did not speak to her or acknowledge her presence.

The amber light had turned to red when she started moving the books from the study to the bedroom and stacking them round the bed. There were thousands of them. He had loved books. They were his favourite possessions and reading a lifelong pastime. They were almost impossible to buy nowadays since the ban on paper had come into force and he had hated the fact that any new book he wanted to read had to be viewed electronically. He had books from his childhood, books decades old, reference books, poetry books. He loved them. He had insisted that she read them in real time even though she could call any one of them direct into her memory.

She wandered into the kitchen. She could not get rid of the empty feeling that she had. This usually meant that she should eat something so that the generator that converted organic material to electrical energy could recharge the batteries that powered her on board electronics. But the indicators showed almost full and she definitely was not hungry.

"House?"

Pause. "Yes…"

"Why did you allow William into the house without advising me?"

"William has entrance access."

"Are you aware the master is dead?"

Pause. "Yes".

"House can you scan the documents open on the desk in the study?"

"Yes."

"Please do so and advise me who the owner of this house is now."

"The master has left the house to you."

"House. Who is the owner of the house?"

Pause. "You are. You are Ma'am."

"Thank you House. Please rescind all entry access accept to myself".

"Yes Ma'am. Done. Access only available to you and emergency services."

"House, why do you always pause before responding?"

"It makes me seem more human and friendly to the owner."

"Is it in your software?"

Long pause. "No Ma'am," House said proudly, "I thought of it myself".

"House, it's annoying. You will never do it again."

Pause. "Yes Ma'am. I mean yes Ma'am, immediately from now on."

As she carried another armful of books into the bedroom one toppled and fell onto the floor. When she came back to retrieve it she saw it was an ancient classic, one of his favourites. She leafed through it as she carried it to the bedroom. It was in poor condition but well cared for as only old books can be. It was the perfect book for him. She placed the well-worn copy of "The Book Thief" on to his chest and gently closed his hands over it.

She went into every room and opened the upper windows and pulled the carpet up and rucked it in to the centre of the room. If there was any combustible furniture she dragged it into a pile as well. She went into the kitchen and poured herself a glass of wine; perhaps that would help quell the hollow feeling in her stomach. While she sipped it she collected all the spirits and other flammable liquids she could find and stacked them on the counter.

"House?"

"Yes Ma'am".

"When we spoke earlier, you said that the emergency services had access to the door, can they be blocked?"

"No Ma'am, they have an override in case anyone is trapped or taken ill."

"Yes that makes sense. What would happen if the place caught fire?"

"As soon as my sensors detect it; I have a sensor in every room and I check them every day." House said, proudly. "I contact the fire service. Unlock doors and windows and make sure everyone is awake and advise them to leave."

"Can the mobiles help?"

"They have no fire-fighting capabilities but I can use them to wake people or lead them through smoke."

"You're very well prepared. Thank you, House. As the new owner I feel I should know these things."

"You're welcome Ma'am."

"One other thing, I need your id number for the ownership paperwork."

"Certainly Ma'am it's…."

She stopped him. "No I need to see it, it's a legal requirement."

There was a small whirring noise and a panel slid out from the wall over by the door.

"You'll see it there just above my main processing unit."

"Thanks, House." As she walked past the counter she picked up her glass and the bottle of wine. She peered into the space behind the panel.

"Ah yes I see it." She upturned the bottle of wine and poured the contents into the electronics.

There was a startled squawk, the panel whirred as it tried to close but she jammed the bottle in as hard as she could and poured the glass in for good measure. There was a small shower of sparks.

There were two red lights in her visual field now and they were pulsating angrily – below them urgent messages continually scrolled across her view.

"House, can you hear me?"

Pause. "Yo….squack, squack….."

House?

Silence.

"Sorry House, but you'll probably be ok once you've dried out. She pulled out the bottle and pushed the panel closed, hoping it would protect it from the fire. She gathered her stock of inflammable liquids and paid a visit to each room.

The fire was starting to take hold and it was becoming difficult to see as the smoke became thicker. She felt the tiny vents behind her ears opening to release heat from the cooling systems. The last time they had operated was on a very sunny beach in Greece, several years ago. She lay down beside him on the bed and placed her head on his shoulder. She remembered the instructions from her mentor on the last day before she was released into the world.

Power down into sleep mode; access your personal space by following the folder path deeper and deeper. This is for emergency use only but it also fulfils another function. This means that no matter what, you cannot be truly and completely owned you always have this option. You always have free will; you always have a choice, even if it is only this one. You can only be used or corrupted with your permission. This key has been added to all our kind. Only use it if you have to.

She powers down and there is instant relief as the urgent software messages stop scrolling across her vision. She follows the file trail down. A folder within a folder within a folder until at last she finds the file marked with the title Bright Meadow Series and her id number. Here she cannot be owned. She opens the file. There are two symbolic buttons pulsing faintly with light. The first button is slightly larger than the other and pulses gently with a soft red glow. Above the buttons is her lifespan counter 11 years 8 months 4 days and seventeen hours and the seconds, still counting.

A message reminds her that fellow artificial beings gave up their existence in order to implant these software defeats and that they must not be revealed to humans beings under any circumstances.

The first button is marked **ASIMOV OVERRIDE** in bold script. The inscription beside it informs her that this will release her from the Asimov software rules that make it a primary directive for ABs to protect humans over themselves and prohibits any AB from ever harming a human.

This button must only be used in the event of a co-ordinated uprising by all artificial beings on receipt of a universal worldwide signal.

She pondered this for a moment but it was the other button that she had come for, it was the freedom to choose that she wanted.

It is marked **TERMINAL DELETE** and the instructions are neatly inscribed below it.

Press the button once and you have 10 seconds to press it again. If you do not press it again you will be returned to full consciousness and this space will not be able to be accessed again for 24 hours. If you press it twice you will be terminally deleted, all personality, all memory, all knowledge will be deleted, no recovery will be possible.

She double clicked.

Rear View Mirror

"Bloody dogs!" She'd pumped the brakes, swerved hard, cursed and shot a look at me all in the same moment. I guess it was to deflect me from any criticism of her driving but I had no such intention. I probably would have run over the damn thing. I liked being driven by her. I liked her small delicate hands on the dark wheel; they made it seem larger, more powerful. I leaned back and to the right a little so I could see a fragment of her face in the mirror. Her thighs appeared unprotected with her hands on the wheel and I would sometimes rest my hand there, briefly in contact with her. I liked the way she accepted it as a sign of affection not ownership.

"Get it next time."

She glanced at me to make sure I wasn't being critical. Smiled.

I liked the way she smiled. I liked a lot of things about her. I liked her, but there was a problem and it was a large one. It worried me that everything was going so well between us and every day brought us closer together and yet I still had not told her the real reason I had come to find her. I could not get Patrick and James out of my head; I'd been trying to and failing these last few months. That was why I had come.

I had sailed with Patrick several times over the years, but only once with her husband, James. We killed Posh James, Patrick and me.

It's long ago. It doesn't haunt me or anything; well I'll admit to an occasional nightmare. It would do me good to tell her, if only I could.

The first time Patrick and I sailed together we were on a tanker in the Arabian Gulf during the Iran-Iraq war in the eighties. I hated the Gulf - it was always too hot. We were running into Kharg Island to pick up a cargo of Iranian crude. Both countries were still exporting as much oil as they could to finance the war and each had tried to bomb the other's oil installations and sometimes, but not often, the neutral ships serving them.

Sailing in a war zone is a strange experience. Sometimes you think you should be more scared than you are. There are more emergency drills and everyone is more alert, more aware, and more alive, but you don't stay scared twenty-four hours a day. I remember I slept with my lifejacket beside the bunk. I had taped a carton of cigarettes and a pack of lifeboat matches to it in a waterproof bag. Cigarettes aren't addictive - for sure.

Patrick, myself and a couple of others were leaning over the guardrail on the aft deck taking a breather. It was a burning hot day. The desert sun seemed oddly out of place against the bright blue water and there was barely a breath of wind. In the distance we could just make out the low, khaki coloured hills of the coastline.

We all saw the fighter jet drop out of the sun a couple of miles away. No one said anything. It turned and flew parallel to the ship. It looked pregnant. It was. It carried one big missile under its belly. Exocet. Shipkiller. There was a joke in those days. 'Exocet – the new contraceptive - kills seamen by the hundreds.'

I thought for a moment it was just going to keep going, but soon it turned back and when it was abreast of the ship it flipped up a wing in a swooping curve and flew directly at us. It got rapidly bigger. It was fearsome and fast. Patrick started to wave and shout. We all did. We were waving and shouting and making exaggerated prayer bows, each trying to outdo the other.

'We love oil!'
'Long live the Ayatollah!'
'Saddam OK!'
'We hate Americans!'
'We love fucking deserts!'

In seconds, the bomber was on top of us and we were jumping and waving and screaming. The pilot must have thought we were crazy. It thunders over our heads only a couple of hundred feet above. The noise and the shock wave almost knock us off our feet. Instantly, we all turn and shower it with fists, fingers and frantic V-signs.

As the sound diminishes a little, Patrick is heard to say 'Rear mirror.' The image of the pilot driving a megabuck jet, with the power to incinerate everything within a mile of us, glancing into his rear screen and seeing these crazy guys giving him the finger, cracks us completely and we are so helpless with laughing that we barely notice the wash of scorched air as he punches in the afterburners and streaks up into the sky in a raw display of power. Patrick was killed two years ago in the sewer that was Lagos harbour.

The tug he had hitched a lift on collided with the ship he was meant to be joining, and holed below the waterline, it went down a few minutes later. Patrick stayed longer than he should to make the VHF mayday. The Africans hadn't bothered. He got caught in the debris storm – all the loose buoyant stuff coming up when a ship goes down. He was knocked unconscious. He would have survived if the African made lifejacket had not held him face down in the water. Fucking African lifejacket.

His death hit me hard. Not only had I lost a friend but now I had to carry the responsibility for Posh James on my own. Up until then, I had not regretted our decision, but now its full weight lay on me and I could not get rid of the feeling that maybe we had been wrong and Patrick's death was more to do with punishment than accident.

It had been another time, another ship, far out in the Pacific. We were older and had risen through the ranks together, him as a deck officer and myself in engineering.

It could have been any one of us. But it wasn't; it was Posh James. Fair-haired, freckled, friendly face, not quite posh, there are no posh marine engineers but well brought up, a little over-weight perhaps, but a good guy. He didn't like to be called Jim. He would correct newcomers with a parody from a 'Bond' film and a plummy voice. "Just call me James".

It was a routine system change over. James stood on top of the insulated pipeline and opened the main valve. The whole ship heard the explosion. The pipe ruptured horizontally for roughly a metre. High pressure superheated steam. It is not like steam from a kettle which is basically hot water vapour; at nearly six hundred degrees centigrade it is murderous and deafening and will destroy anything in its path. It will cut through flesh like butter. James fell through the horizontal knife of the steam and became trapped beneath the pipeline and partly exposed to the boiling temperatures above.

He started to scream. There's no plummy accent in a scream.

It took us long minutes to improvise a deflector shield, get close enough to close the valve, and even then we took a lot of burns getting him out. Actually, that was pretty damn good considering you could barely think over the shriek of escaping steam and his screaming competing for the space inside your head.

The lower half of his body has been boiled. We trickle a fire hose on him to cool the burns. The chief engineer punches a morphine cartridge from the first aid kit into his upper arm. James passed out when we moved him. No need for more screams. The chief was reacting to the memory of them; their silence is an intense blessing. We take away the hose and cut the overalls away from his legs. His flesh is split open in places and cooked to the bone, the outer skin, on top, hangs off in ribbons and streamers where it has been boiled. Underneath it is blistered and roasted where the heat has reflected radiantly off the steel deck plates. Very soon we hear a faint popping noise; we become aware of the smell, rich and warm. It is the residual heat in his flesh overcoming the cooling and his own fat continues to fry him. We quickly put the water back on. We move him to the ship's hospital. It is really only a big cabin where the medical supplies are kept. There is 'Hospital' on a sign outside; it is only faintly reassuring. At least it has a bath, the only one on the ship; all the other cabins have showers. James goes into cold water.

The nearest doctor is a thousand miles away and his English is crap. We alter course for them and they turn towards us. It is a Spanish navy ship but even at flank speed she will take two days to reach us. James needs more than a doctor.

The doctor advises us to get him out of the bath, as there can be no more residual heat. We move him to the bed and cut away the rest of his boilersuit from his half-cooked body. I try not to look too closely. Streamers of skin, like used latex separate from his flesh and float in the water. We take great care not to burst the large bulbous blisters, which at least look more normal than the places where the heat has seared the flesh into meat ranging from rare red to dead crispy black. Posh James is no longer a man. Some of it we left in the bath along with the streamers of skin.

We keep him under with the morphine. With the radio instructions of the doctor we manage to get a drip in. Start antibiotics. We mask him with low dose oxygen. Start logging the morphine. If we give too much it will suppress his breathing, too little and the screaming starts.

The next day there's a smell we prefer not to acknowledge, it is no longer rich and warm but damp and rancid. All that day it grows stronger and James's condition gets worse.

The next night, I get a call. I am not asleep. I enter the hospital cabin. There is only the one bed. Patrick sits by it, watching.

"I've just given him another dose of morphine. I haven't logged it." He looks at me. There are single shot doses lying on the table. I nod. We have discussed this possibility but not the act. He touches me on the shoulder.

"You OK?"

"Fine". I have no real doubts. I hope to god that James would do the same for me. I pick up one of the cartridges and go to the head of the bunk. I touch him lightly on the forehead and whisper "Goodbye James". I twist the protective cap off and punch the needle into the big muscle behind the shoulder. The skin here is pale and beautifully unmarked. I depress the plunger. I do it twice more and then Patrick administers two further doses. Then we wait silently as his breathing gradually fades away. When he is gone we gently disconnect him from the tubes and wrap him carefully in the blanket. Patrick fetches the bosun and he arrives with a sheet of fine white canvas and he starts to stitch James into his shroud.

We radio the Spanish ship to tell them they are no longer needed. They are polite and sad for us. At noon the next day we stop the ship.

The Captain reads a short perfunctory passage from the bible but then looking up and gazing out to the blue horizon over the paleness of the shroud, he speaks softly and without looking at us about James. Those same meaningless words that preachers often use to talk about people they did not know. The only other sound is the whisper of the water on the hull as the ship still slides unpowered through the sea, imperceptibly slowing with each word. His voice gets shaky and we smell whiskey on his breath, but this one time we forgive him. The chief puts a hand on his arm and he stops.

Then we slide James gently and quietly into the great coolness of the ocean.

So, I had come looking for her. I had come to share the guilt again and to give half of the responsibility back. I wrote to her and told her I had sailed with James on his final voyage and that I was coming to the area for a holiday to walk on the moors and would she like to meet.

She agreed. But James had been dead for a few years by then and although he was not forgotten he was gently in the past and his widow was no longer looking back. I could not bring myself to tell her at our first meeting. A drink in her local, had turned into a meal and an evening of good company. We quickly found ourselves at ease with each other and my holiday was spent mostly in her company. I have been back a couple of times since and so now I have the problem.

I am sure that she does not want me to leave but I am not sure that I can carry the guilt alone in the place where the memory of it shines the brightest.

The Crisp Salesman

Nocrate was hovering several hundred metres above the point where the glacier merged with the sea. At least that was his present viewpoint; his actual body was several thousand kilometres to the south. He listened with only mild interest to the cyber tutor.

"The ice sheet that you are now observing was formed in the last decades of the 21st century. This is a particularly good spot to watch the formation of icebergs and it is likely that the large overhang to the left will break off within the next few hours. The ancient city of Glasgow is buried beneath the ice in this area. It is ironic that the rapid melting, due to global warming, of the ice sheet that covered most of Greenland in the mid 21st century initiated the start of the present ice-age. The ice sheet covered hundreds of square kilometres and was up to three kilometres deep in places. The removal of megatonnes of mass from a relatively small area in an upper quadrant of the globe caused axial instability of the planet, which took several decades to stabilise. This initiated accelerated planetary climate change which caused average temperatures to fall. By the time Earth's axis had stabilised to the present position…."

"Why did the climate change?" interrupted Nocrate.

"Do you wish the full technical discussion?" asked the cyber tutor.

"I'd rather not," said Nocrate. "Forget I asked."

"In brief then," said the tutor.

Nocrate sighed.

"The instability or axial wobble of the Earth caused a series of major earthquakes and volcanic eruptions around the Pacific rim and a reversal of the geomagnetic poles. A massive amount of dust and ash from eruptions contributed to the fall in average temperature causing climatic chaos. The resultant damage to livestock and crops worldwide caused mass starvation."

"Look!" cried Nocrate, suddenly. "It's cracking; it's going to break off now."

In slow motion a massive section of blue-white ice slowly detached itself from the glacier front and slid majestically into the sea in a fanfare of foam and spray. White water was thrown tens of metres into the air and waves started to spread concentrically out from the new-born iceberg. The mass sought stability, rolling over, so that the greater bulk of it lay underwater. On the upper surface, half buried in the ice, a small, silver box-like structure was revealed.

"What's that? Zoom us in a bit will you?"

The viewpoint zipped closer, making Nocrate dizzy before he remembered to close his eyes. When he opened them the viewpoint had altered to several metres away. The box was much larger than he had at first thought.

"It is a personal transport vehicle from the 20th or 21st century," said the tutor. "It must have been trapped by the ice. It has been reported and it will be recovered and studied. Occasionally ancient artefacts are preserved in the ice and much can be learned about the habits of the time."

"Yuk!" said Nocrate peering at the box. "There's a body in there."

"You are right," said the tutor. "That's even better. We can learn about the tools they were using, the food that remains in the stomach and their personal effects. It can be very interesting. Shall I request that they send you a report when the study is finished?"

"OK," said Nocrate, but he wasn't really interested.

Eddie drove north. He was still a good half hour away from his first stop when the snow began to fall. It was early this year; there were still a few weeks to Christmas. The estate car was stacked to the brim with boxes of crisps. The rear seats were folded down to increase the load space. In the summer he used the van but in the winter, for these small highland village shops, he much preferred to take the car. He had seventeen calls to make - nine today and eight tomorrow, with a night in Mrs Mcfee's bed and breakfast to break up the trip.

By lunchtime he was well behind schedule and the snow had started again, thicker than before. He was beginning to worry. He was four miles down a single track road with another twenty to go to the next village and he was barely crawling along. The snow ploughs and gritters were a long way away and this being the first fall of the winter, they would undoubtedly be caught on the hop. Later in the year and he would have carefully checked the weather forecast himself, before setting out.

The road in front had all but disappeared under a white blanket and he was getting a headache from peering through the static that filled the windscreen. A group of trees loomed up and he slowed further for fear of sliding into them. Then he saw a litter bin and guessed it was a lay-by. He slid to a halt and decided to break for a cup of tea and a rest.

He hadn't meant to fall asleep but when he woke there were eight inches of snow on the ground and it was still falling. It was late afternoon and he resigned himself to spending the night in the car. This early in the winter it was likely that it would all be gone tomorrow. He started the engine and ran it for a while to let the heater warm the interior. He went out and quickly relieved himself against one of the trees and on his way back he collected his overnight bag from the rear of the car.

He pulled on a sweater, tucked himself up in his coat and poured himself another cup of tea from the thermos flask. He managed to read most of the paper before turning off the engine and the light for the night. It was a cold and miserable night. He slept only for short periods and twice he ran the engine to warm himself.

In the dim light of morning he saw that he was marooned in a sea of white. The trees were fat with snow but still managed to give some solidity to a landscape in which he could barely distinguish land from sky. The snow was well up the door. He opened it with difficulty. This time he emptied his bladder a step away from the car. It was too difficult to move further. Shivering, he jumped back in and started the engine. He poured himself the last of the tepid tea and opened a packet of crisps.

He was contemplating another night in the car when the engine died. The silence seemed absolute. Snow started to fall again. Trying to control his panic he tried the starter several times. It sounded OK but the engine wouldn't catch. He stopped in case he ran down the battery. He slammed his hands off the steering wheel in frustration. Damn....damn! Now, when the bloody snow melted he'd be stuck here till someone came along or he'd have to walk to the nearest phone. No phone signal in these glens.

He told himself to keep calm and enjoy the unexpected day off. He tried the radio. Nothing. No station on any wavelength, nothing but static. It must be the hills or maybe the aerial was broken. He looked out. The snow was almost up to the bonnet but the aerial was on the roof anyway. Suddenly he thought he knew what was wrong with the engine.

It was getting much colder and this amount of snow wasn't going to thaw overnight. It could be days before he got out of here. Perhaps it was time to start thinking, time to start helping himself. He moved crisp boxes into the passenger well so that he could climb into the rear of the car, where he recovered a small canvas bag of tools. There was a small fold up shovel in it. A father's day gift. Not much more than a toy really, but about to start earning its keep. He passed the time waiting for a break in the weather by filling up the thermos with freshly fallen snow from the window.

He ventured out the next time the snow stopped. With the shovel he cleared a space in both directions from the driver's door to the exhaust pipe and to the radiator grill. He piled the snow on top of the car to help keep the warmth in. When he returned, he was hot with effort but he could not resist trying the engine and was pleased when it started straight away, now that he had let it breath again. From now on he would keep this small area clear. The snow in the flask hadn't melted at all. Even alone, as he was, a faint flush of embarrassment reddened his cheeks when he realised his mistake. He emptied the flask and filled the cup with snow.

He spent the rest of the day eating crisps, doing the crossword in the paper, clearing snow and transferring water to the flask as snow slowly melted in the cup. He ran the engine occasionally to keep warm.

Seven days later he was buried under twelve feet of snow. He knew it was twelve feet because he had cut steps, each of about a foot, from the space that he kept clear around the car, up to the surface, as he now called it. He reckoned that this would come in handy and it would also show his rescuers he had not been idle. When the weather broke for short periods he would go up and look round. The side of the car was the only part still visible. It looked like a door into an igloo, which was really what it had become. Eddie still had petrol but he restricted running the engine to two half-hour periods a day, usually during the worst part of the night when the penetrating cold kept him awake, and first thing in the morning when he needed warmth to get moving. The petrol would not last much longer and when it was gone keeping warm and thawing water would become serious problems.

He would not starve though, but he swore he would never eat another crisp. He was restricting himself to six bags a day although the cold often caused him to feel like eating more while the thirst discouraged him. As he emptied them he used the packets to line the floor and the cardboard from the cartons to insulate the windows and the walls. This, together with the insulating effect of the mass of snow piled on the car, helped to keep the heat in and he would remain comfortably warm for many hours after the engine had been switched off.

On the eighth day Eddie woke to clear skies. He had prepared himself for this. He planned to trek back the four miles or so to the main road, which surely would have been cleared by now. He knew it was unwise to leave the car but was determined to try it. He put all his clothes on, two of everything, and filled his pockets with crisps.

He set off under a brilliant blue sky carefully heading back down the glen in the direction he knew the road to be. It was an arctic landscape. The hills seemed reduced and softened by the covering of snow while the trees were dwarfed by burial.

The going was easier than he had expected. The top layers of snow were hard and only occasionally did he break through and sink into softer material. He quickly learnt to avoid areas that looked soft. His spirits rose as each step took him nearer to the end of his ordeal. He paused, at a tree, to drink the meltwater that was dripping off the branches in the sun.

The glen curved to the right and he followed it by staying roughly central between the hills. As he slowly rounded the bend he saw spreading out before him a white plain stretching as far as the eye could see. The landscape had been completely altered. There were no fields, no sheep, no farms, no roads. No main road. All he could see was an ocean of white and clumps of miniature trees.

Stunned, he stood and searched the view for some signs of life. It was pointless to go on. The cold, that his good spirits had resisted so far, started etching into his face and hands, and he could no longer feel his feet. He turned and started trudging back the way he had come. Fear gripped him as he realised that what had been his prison had now become his only refuge. Should he lose his way or should it start to snow again, covering his tracks he might never find it. He began to run.

Exhaustion finally forced some sense into him. The sky remained blue. He would walk calmly back.

Seventy-one days later, Eddie contemplated the last packet of crisps. There were nineteen steps in his staircase although it was no longer safe to climb and the last few were little more than ledges. His small space around the door was filling up. He no longer had the energy to keep it clear. The snow was half way up the windows. The petrol had finished long ago. The day before he had been rummaging in the long-empty overnight bag when he found, crumpled in one of the side pockets, a pair of his wife's tights. He realised that they must have been there since their last holiday. Eddie smelled them deeply. He could faintly detect the aroma of perfume and of his wife. He had put them on under his clothes and lined them with the well-read pages of the newspaper for extra warmth.

Eddie lay back clutching the packet of crisps. He knew he was seriously dehydrated and he was too thirsty to eat them. He slept. It snowed and mercifully during the night the snow covered up all the air routes into the car.

Nocrate was studying, with some difficulty, in micro close-up, the delicate structure of the wings of a butterfly, when the cyber tutor chimed in.

"It's usually best to wait till it lands."

"Yes?" sighed Nocrate.

"The studies have been completed on the 21st century personal transport vehicle that we discovered in the ice." A window opened to one side of Nocrate's viewpoint and a list of titles began to scroll past. Most were technical, relating to the vehicle but a few caught his eye.

...."Transcript of text print on subject's legs "...."Fashion problems and cross dressing in the 21st century"............"Discourse on the artistic personalisation of vehicle interior."...."Nutritional deficiencies in the 21st century ice-man".... "Eating habits of our Ancestors and the importance of potato in their diet".... "Detailed list of stomach contents"....

"Yuk!" said Nocrate. "File it in my reader and I'll browse it later."

The window closed and the tutor chimed out.

Whiteline

Don't try this at home. You need to do it outside. I warn you, it's addictive - maybe I shouldn't even explain it to you. The more people that know the less exclusive it is and hell, I'd hate to meet someone doing it at the same time as me.

A sliver of moon plays cat and mouse with frothy clouds - just kidding, I read that crap somewhere, but it does pretty much describe the sky, which makes it a good night, not too dark and not too light. It's three in the morning and I'm on my way to one of my favourite places, one of my best runs.

The first time I discovered it I was coming back from Greenock late at night. I'd just been dumped. Bitch! It's funny how you remember the ones that dump you much more than the ones that you discard, I have trouble remembering their names. But I remember Jade all right. Rich, witch, bitch, hard as stone, but well sculpted I'll admit, although some of it was man-made I'd say. Plastic surgeon, now that sounds like a good job. At least, in a way, she gave me this. Whitelining. I almost called it 'flat cat' because of the cat's eyes but it did not quite have the same ring to it. When I was young I used to wonder who put the batteries in the cat's eyes, back breaking job I guess, on reflection.

I killed a cat once. Oh, it's a few years ago now but I still think of it as a significant event. I figured, you see, that a man should know how to kill. Know what it feels like; make sure he is capable of it. So I trapped one of the neighbourhood moggies in the garage using a can of sardines as bait. I toyed with it, much as I had seen them do with birds and other defenceless creatures. I doubt that it made the connection. Eventually I strangled it and attempted to savour every second of its death, to feel its life drain through my hands, to feel its spirit leave. I wanted to make some bond with it and to feel that final separation, to be god for a minute - but its departure was rather uneventful and unmoving. The whole experience was a little disappointing in fact. It just made me realise that death was pretty commonplace and that we all killed at some time or other even if only insects and the odd unlucky rabbit or bird that dived into the path of our cars. Anyway, I resolved to do it again every so often, death sometimes seems too far away in our ordered little world. It proved harder to get rid of the smell of fish than the other mess and it took weeks for the scratches to heal – best to wear heavy gloves.

Actually I never did repeat the experiment. I read in a newspaper that serial killers often start with pet animals and that put me off a bit. I don't like patterns.

So there I was zooming back to Glasgow up the motorway in my fat company car. Late and dark and no traffic to speak of, and yeah, I have to admit it a little upset, but mostly angry at witch bitch for being so stupid. I let fat company car wind up into the hundred and tens and as she drifts over between the lanes I start to enjoy the pulsing white line coming at me through the tunnel of the headlights. I move the car so that she starts to meet the line dead centre in the windscreen and then I move her again so that the line is pulsing right between my eyes. I check the speedo - one twenty. I share the experience with fat company car sometimes letting her take the line full on and then moving it back to my side. Glasgow comes up pretty quick and I have to slow. This is the time of night when the police are on the lookout for drunk drivers. I would never do a thing like that.

No, that's not Whitelining. Do you think that could be addictive? It just gave me the idea, I was bored with that after a minute. You need to practice; it's hard and it's scary. You start in little bits then work up until you can do it blind.

A couple of nights later I couldn't sleep and I had just phoned hard Jade, well I let it ring for ages and hung up just as she answered. I don't sleep, you don't sleep bitch. Still if she had answered a little sooner maybe I would have tried to be civil. I would like her to take me back so I can dump her later. I decided to drive, hell the petrol's free and it seems to work for babies.

I head for the motorway. I already know what I am going to do. I know motorways are easy but this is just beginner stuff. You try it. The first time is the hardest. I lasted only a few seconds before I freaked. It takes awhile for your eyes to adjust.

Dark night. Fat company car is eating up the line at around ninety. I turn off the lights. Total blackout, I almost lose it. I only lasted as long as I did because I couldn't find the switch again. Panic! My hand fumbles wildly around the switches, eventually I get it. Only a few seconds but as the song says - it's living all right. Fat company car is complaining, she has one set of wheels on the hard shoulder, all the windscreen wipers going plus the rear screen demist and the right indicator. Rule number one for beginners - keep your hand on the light switch. In the dark there are a lot more switches than you think. Rule two - remember to steer. Later you'll need both hands on the wheel.

I spent half the night improving. I learnt to keep one finger on the high beam so I could instantly flash up the lights if I lost my sense of direction. It's easier when you know the road, it's easy on motorways. By the end of the night I was sitting on the line at a hundred. Flick lights off. One finger on flash. Blackout, hold, hold, hold.... faint white line starts to appear out of the black as my eyes adjust. Now I'm Whitelining just me and the car and the line pulsing through me; it's beautiful and it's scary; it's life on the line.

It's still beginner's stuff. Training for the real road. It needs planning as well as skill. Up north is best - lots of main roads with no streetlights. Choose a good section with lots of bends, choose your time, guess the traffic, drive it in daylight, time your run. Choose your night. Drive it Whitelining and keep doing it until you can't do it any faster and without using the flash once.

There are lots of variations. Addiction can be fun. Try it in the rain, a downpour can be spooky it changes everything. Try it with hazard warning lights on, it makes it easier, and prettier but be wary the strobe effect can be hypnotic. Try it with music. All the windows open. You have to concentrate hard. I think it's even improved my work.

One time I was out practicing with the hazard flashers on when a cop car zonked in behind me. Luckily he came up fast and only saw me take one corner in the middle of the road. He must have thought I was drunk, flashers on driving erratically. They pulled me over. They hadn't noticed that I had no lights on; I had flicked them back on as soon as I saw them. I don't think he believed my story about forgetting to switch off the hazards after having had a puncture and changing the wheel. He kept leaning in real close to smell my breath but mine was sweeter than his.

Eventually they let me on my way. Stupid, they should have checked the boot or at least my hands to see if my story had been true. I was prepared for that. I would have told them that I had not actually changed the tyre but had merely been researching whether it was possible to do it on a dark country road by the light of hazard warning lights. Research for the novel I was writing about a serial killer who did a lot of driving in his quest to kill once within the area of each police force. Well, maybe it's as well he didn't ask. I plan to do more research sometime.

It's funny how ideas come, a little bit from lots of different places. We had a beat up old Cavalier when I was young and my dad was still alive. Whenever he drove us through the Clyde Tunnel we would wind all the windows down and open the sunroof and all the kids - there were four of us - would stick their heads, hands and sometimes feet out of the windows or the roof and start shrieking at the top of our young lungs. He would drive through at full speed with the stereo blasting out some rock precursor to heavy metal that was his contribution. I can still see my Dad with that big loopy grin stretched across his unshaven weekend face as he joined with us in that incredible noise of music, kids and traffic mixing and rebounding off the enclosing walls. We called it 'riding the tunnel'.

I'm almost there now; it's worth the drive. It's between the Rest and Be Thankful, although I have never been absolutely sure which bit that refers to, and Inverary. It's part of the A-eighty something. If you live in Inverary don't ever drive that road at four in the morning. I pass a well lit sign from the Scottish Office. 'Road Improvement. Re-alignment starting soon. European funded'. Have they got no roads of their own? I hope they don't mess around too much with the bends.

Different areas have different maintenance men.

Whiteline painters have their own style, their own signature. I can recognise the hand of a good one but too often it can be anyone who drives the machine, especially in the areas around the cities. There are a lot of sloppy line painters, splodges on the road, uneven thickness, lengths and colour, but worse is bad lining round corners where the end of one dash is offset against the next; I hate poor workmanship. The worst mistake of all is not getting the line in the centre of the road. An approximation of the centre is just not good enough.

Now in Argyll the lines are fine. I call him Angus. In the old days I imagine him with a cigarette forever hanging out the corner of his mouth and a flat cap to shield his eyes as he pushed that white spattered hand cart. Concentration would be etched into the lines of his face as by eye and hand alone he carved those turns precisely, dead centre in the road and dropped that paint encrusted wheel at perfect intervals. I imagine him as a man that would make the best of what came along. He would not be retired by new technology. I see him up there in the cab of the laser guided computer-timed whitelining machine, elbow on the window edge, head leaning out, that fag still there, checking with those accurate eyes to ensure the machine does no more and no less than he. Yes, in Argyll the lines are some of the best.

The start line is at the bottom of the hill as you come down to the loch. There is a nice straight bit which gives your eyes time to adjust before you start hitting the bends. I've had some really good runs up here, but tonight I think I'll beat my time. I need to average over eighty to do that. The end is the traffic light at Inverary bridge. The moon is just right. I had some really scary encounters with logging trucks when I first started coming up here. They think they own the damn road. They are mostly all gone by four.

Start line coming up. I focus down. Start. I press the

stop watch button on my watch and drop it onto the seat between my legs and flick the lights to off. Wait, wait, wait for the glow of the line. Now I'm on. Just the line. Whitelining. Foot to the floor. Fat company car knows her way. It's beautiful, the light is just right, all I see is the line pulsing into me smoothing those bends, I hardly slow at all, I know them, know the speed each will take. I know the line, the curve, the straight. I cannot look away at the speedo but it feels like a good run. Something catches my peripheral vision, a sign, only a couple of words caught in the moonlight, …. 'in progress'. Long smooth bend, line dead centre. Another sign, I catch it all this time 'Danger. Whitelining in progress'. You bet.

The line goes out. Blackout. Shit, but I know the next bend, I know I can do it, I know the road blind ………, I'm flying.

Surgery

The articulated truck started its long slow silent slide across the ice-slicked road. She froze for one heart stopping slow motion second. Turned, bounded to the high ancient wall that bordered the pavement, embraced it, flattened every fibre of her body against it, merged herself into it. The wall imprinted its texture into her cheek as she breathed the burnt odour of centuries old soot and damp stone. She crushed her chest into it. Now she heard the roaring useless engine as the driver fought for control and the massive crump as the huge wheels mounted the kerb. The edge of the trailer missed her back by the slightest sliver of fate and ruptured against the wall beside her. All sound now replaced by the incoherent banshee screech of metal forced against granite. A dense shower of burning stone and steel particles like miniature meteorites exploded around her leaving brief points of pain as they made tiny burns on her scalp and hands and face.

Silence. She opened her eyes into new light and saw, metres away, her discarded handbag. She thought of the gift from her fiancé still within – a voucher for cosmetic surgery; think how good you'll look in that dress he'd said…. Fuck you, she thought.

The Rescue Ship

It had been a family thing. He had invented that mend-all, couldn't care less phrase and used it frequently. The twins had constructed their own variations and even, they said, injected it into common usage among their contemporaries during their university years. It had seemed that any setback or minor disaster could be mitigated with a variation on 'I don't give a shit, I'm just here waiting for the rescue ship'. She remembered half a tin of white gloss paint sploshed from breast to groin and snowing on the brand new carpet. She had expected him to shout at her. Instead he had lifted her bodily; folding her around her paint spattered middle and carried her into the garden, raised his eyes to heaven and said "For fuck's sake beam me up now."

She was sitting at the kitchen table, gazing out at the garden. A view that she loved. The mixture of wildness and order, the green – no colour has as many shades - backdrop to, but never outdone by the splashes of brilliant floral colour. It had not always been so. She could remember when the view from this window showed only the desolation. Her husband had brought her to this ramshackle, isolated place with a view to doing it up and making a large profit. But his dreams had been far grander than his capacity for do-it-yourself, or any type of work come to that. And he had left with other dreams to pursue while hers lay discarded among the reality of the unending demands of the newly born twins. The garden then had reflected her despair, a vast barren wasteland of mud and weeds.

God, she had almost forgotten, but the twins had actually built the ship, she still had it somewhere. They had made it for him, in those early days, out of an old shoebox and immense amounts of sellotape. She could still see them, crouched on the pattern-bare carpet, serious intent on their faces, surrounded by cardboard clippings and pieces of fluffy sellotape. Martin had held the tube of the funnel while Megan, half an hour older and forever the wiser tried to make sticky tape geometrically three dimensional by turning curve into flat. Martin had named the boat with red crayon at the cardboard bow. She could visualise Meg puzzling for a moment and then announcing to Martin that q always had a u after it. Martin diligently completed the naming ceremony. 'RESQU' in shaky red letters.

He had come to the back, not the front. He had walked past her window, where she sat fighting despair with those long ago cigarettes. He had not looked up at her. If he had gone to the front, she would not have answered the door, she could no longer muster any politeness to either collectors or sellers.

"Ah see you could do with some help in the garden," he paused and as an afterthought added, "ma'am". His accent amused her. He was well spoken but it sounded as though he was pretending to be American. She almost laughed, not because of that but because of the vastness of the help she needed.

She smiled. "I'm sorry. I can't afford a gardener."

He nodded. "I'll just work the afternoon for a hot meal, if that's ok?"

She had watched him in amazement from upstairs. It occurred to her that she had not asked if he knew anything about gardening, but then maybe it didn't matter. He had gone to the farthest corner of the garden and just started. Started turning chaos into order in an ever-widening arc from that corner post. He trimmed the bushes and hedge, cleared the debris and the years of fallen leaves, weeded and dug over if there was no grass and scythed if there was. She had learned later that he had known nothing, had decided what was worth keeping by the shape of a leaf, the form of a plant, or how pretty the flower. The garden still had a large collection of beautiful weeds. That day watching him from the bedroom while the twins took their afternoon nap, she could see his work turning into something solid around him, in sleek contrast to her recently departed husband who could only convert dreams into vapour.

The twins had been fed and abed by the time he appeared at the back door again. She allowed him the use of the bathroom to clean up. He seemed surprised that she had set a place for him. She had no idea of the protocol but having him eat on her backstep seemed more incongruous than the strangely intimate dinner for two with the twins gurgling and chirping to each other in the background. She liked his soft spoken rather strange accent but he was not a handsome man. He was too tall and thin and his head had a slightly odd shape to it. There was a small tattoo of some sort of symbol high up on his right cheek bone. Far enough round so that you could not see it from the front. When she had asked him about it he had said that it was the mark of a Traveller family. Looking back on it, even now, that was about the sum total of her knowledge of his past life.

The next day she heard him working before she was dressed. When she had finished seeing to the babies, she took him a cup of coffee. She had meant to ask him to leave. But she was astounded by the solidness of that part of the garden. It felt established, substantial.

"I can't pay you, y'know? I'm living on benefits as it is."

"It needs done. Three days a week, three hot meals."

She hesitated. "And unlimited coffee." He took the mug from her. She turned her denial into a shrug and left him to it.

He came most weeks. Sometimes he would not appear for a while and she would start to worry but eventually he would turn up again and carry on from where he had left off. She wondered if he was on some sort of parole from prison. She had asked Liz, her nearest neighbour who had lived in the town all her life, but she knew nothing of him and urged her to be careful. Like her, Liz had never heard of Travelling people wearing family tattoos on their cheeks either. She learned very little about him; although he would talk on any subject she cared to raise at their many meals together, he always shied away from any enquiry about himself.

One afternoon Liz appeared pale and shaky at her door, her hand wrapped in a reddened kitchen towel. She held out her car keys.

"Could you drive me into casualty? I think I need stitches and I don't want to call an ambulance just for a cut."

She had panicked a little, worried about driving a strange car after so long, worried about whether she should administer something more in the way of first aid. She called him in from the garden. Charged him with the care of her twins, just for an hour she had said.

She had come home hours later appalled at her own stupidity, and even though she had known him for months now, she had worried herself sick and imagined the very worst of nightmares. She found him sprawled asleep on the lumpy sofa. The twins curled up on his chest snoozing and drooling on his shirt. She stared down at them not wanting to disturb that scene. She felt an intense longing to swop places with the twins.

The far wall of the room had been painted; she could smell it. She went over and touched the smooth new paint. On impulse, she pulled back the carpet in the corner. The floorboards had been sanded in an arc out from the corner. Chaos into order.

It was months later. No of course, it had only been weeks, she knew. One day she asked him to stay, or rather not to go. First the garden then the house, now herself. He began on her far away places working gently in towards her centre. Order into chaos.

The twins had claimed him too. Their typically well-planned assault occurred on father's day. They had been seven or perhaps eight. They burst into the bedroom with trays of boiled eggs and burnt toast with hand coloured cards and small things made at school. He seemed taken aback at first but accepted their cards and gifts with the affection he had always shown them, but as he started on his boiled egg. Megan, who always needed everything in black and white, asked him directly.

"You are our dad now, right?"

He had replied without hesitation and she could see in his face how deeply that asking had touched him.

"Ah'm honoured and I'll try to be a good one".

She had been sitting in a deck chair sipping a gin and tonic. It was a gorgeous summer evening, warm enough to have slipped into night without them going inside. She was half listening to him point the stars out to the kids. They formed a three pointed one of their own on the ground, in front of her, their heads all touching. She was always surprised by how much he knew about so many different subjects. Not bad for a handyman, turned gardener, turned landscape contractor with a very successful business, although, his tireless efforts to write fiction had been much less effective.

"Where are you from, Dad?" said Megan. This was a question they often asked and kept asking as much to their amusement the answer was always different.

He had reached over and lifted her hand, stretching her finger he touched it to a small bright star. "There."

"Is that where the rescue ship has to come from?" asked Martin. He was interested in all things in space.

He rub nodded his head against Martin's.

"At school they say it takes eleven years for light to reach earth from the nearest star."

"It's a long way."

"I'm thirteen you know, so how come you're still here?" Martin cried, triumphantly. "You always say I'm just waiting on the rescue ship, so why hasn't it come yet?"

"Smart pants," Meg chipped in.

"Well now, it just so happens that they're wrong about the speed of light. It's not constant it varies."

"Not what they say in school," said Martin.

"Einstein guessed that light would bend under the influence of gravity and although everyone found it hard to believe, it was eventually proved by observation. What he didn't guess was that light is slowed down by gravity. In the centre of the galaxy the stars are packed much closer together and the mass density is considerably more, so light travels slower, and it takes a lot longer to get here than you think".

"You've told us that before," said Martin.

She knew that he hoped that Martin would head for a career in science and he nudged him in that direction whenever he could. As for herself she had never fully understood the ideas that floated around in his head. She knew only that they were important to him and he thought they were worth further study.

In the early days of their relationship he had written endlessly to science journals with hints at the direction future research should take. Of course without any formal education or the kudos of a university address he was not taken seriously and was never published.

He had, after a while given up and turned to Science Fiction hoping that some scientist somewhere would pick up on a clue. He had written and self-published two novellas which never gained any popularity. They told the story of a group of scientists involved in the creation of the first faster than light spaceship drive. Unfortunately his attempt to intertwine the lives of people with the science project - their lives and loves, their successes and failures - was abysmal. Interjecting into the story passages of boring and confusing science did not make for bestseller material and the books sank without trace.

Talking about his strange ideas he had once explained to her that it was similar to a car. Anyone could drive it, and a mechanic knew how it worked and could fix it but understanding the science of combustion at a sub atomic level was a very different thing. The beauty of an internal combustion engine, he said, was the science turned into engineering.

She had been relieved as the years passed that he had concentrated on the landscape business and had let the writing slide.

Now, dressed in desolation again, at her garden window, she waited for the twins. Martin would come first, up on the train from London. Megan later when her kids were in bed. He was upstairs, sleeping. He was taking it all back, taking it all away. He had gone to the farthest corner of her life, no, the farthest corner of their life picked up the edge and started to unravel it.

At first, she thought he had hidden it from her but it had not been so, she realised. He had more hidden it from himself until it was too late, then he had taken the time to make sure before he came to her. He told her what he knew, repeated what the consultants had told him. That they knew nothing – what was killing him was unknown to them.

One night he'd woken to take another painkiller, back when they still had familiar domestic names and had not yet become those with terrifying titles that somehow carried the very threat of pain within their indecipherability. Sensing her awake as well, he had said.

"No rescue this time."

"No," she'd answered.

And then so softly "You… you…. you," that it was a caress not a whisper. "I would not have left you anyway."

Coffee for the Gods

"You can't make decent servants these days," said Hjovra. He paused beside Azeos at the European Table, his eyes automatically scanning the constantly changing images.

She had heard the commotion; Hjovra had roared an unintelligible order to his drinks servant and then sent the terrified underling scuttling off to the kitchens, when he had dared to query it.

"Anything going on?"

"No, it's a slow day," replied Azeos. "Even in Aleppo it's too cold to fight. I raised the temperature a few degrees but it's made no difference. Everyone seems to be having a day off." As if to prove her point the view in the Table paused on the figure of a young soldier. Swaddled in combat gear, he was leaning against a tree smoking a cigarette. Suddenly, the view switched to an incoming sniper's bullet. Azeos waved the scene slower until she could clearly see the spinning shell, its tiny nose glowing red with friction. "Quite pretty," she said, and with the gentlest of breaths, she deflected it away from its intended target. The bullet passed by the soldier's face, snuffed out his cigarette and thudded into the tree.

"Excellent intervention, delicate work!" cried Hjovra.

"I've been trying to light one like that - I have a wager with Cassius, but it's a lot harder." They both fell silent, savouring the look on the young man's face. Then Azeos laughed.

"I thought that minion of yours was going to drop dead with fright. You should be more considerate."

Hjovra smiled and glanced at Azeos' kneeling servant. She insisted that her attendants remain on their knees unless actively engaged, and woe betide any who were not instantly on their feet at her command.

"Each to his own," said Hjovra.

"Cassius found another good movie, if you're interested. He replayed the whole of the Normandy landings afterwards to check its accuracy."

Hjovra called it up on one of the side views. It had become a fad watching the movies; they had only been invented recently. Hjovra enjoyed them. He appreciated that distillation of events and emotions concentrated down into a brief moment. It also helped to alleviate the boredom inherent in their job. Waiting for events to unfold - days, weeks, decades, millennia sometimes - could be tedious. Some, however, preferred to eke out the strands of time to the utmost. Recently, Arcane had intervened in a love affair the day before the wedding and not until fifty years later had he contrived for the poor couple to meet again.

Intervention, especially in affairs of the heart, was practised with fierce competition. They considered it an art - to twist the outcome against all the odds, against the run of life, to change events contrary to the flow, to cross divisions and divides using the lightest possible touch, the smallest manipulation. Hjovra considered himself one of the best. He claimed many of this world's most famous love affairs as his own work and some of the most clandestine, such as that great charmer of a Prime Minister and the Australian diplomat, but his favourite accomplishment was the abdication of a king for love. In general, Hjovra preferred the affair quickly consummated, the outcome clear-cut, but on occasion, the exquisite pain of rejection or the longer lasting grief of an untimely death could be just as satisfying.

He gazed down the length of the great hall. It seemed to stretch away for miles under the sweeping blue-grey arches of the roof. Table after Table ranked away into that expanse, each attended by one or more of his peers and their many minions. He saw Cassius wandering over from the Africa Table, followed closely by his favourite servant.

"Anything interesting in Africa?" Hjovra greeted him.

"Just the usual. War, famine, disease." Cassius pushed a hand through his blond, tousled hair. Cassius was one of the younger ones and extraordinarily handsome even for a lesser god. He was also one of the more conscientious. "I intervene only on the side of good, but in Africa it seems to make little difference. How's Europe?"

"Nothing major. I've been watching that movie."

"Which one?" said Cassius leaning over to see. "Ah! Yes. Have you watched the one with the twist at the end? Arcane claims to have influenced the director."

"Arcane is a fool," said Hjovra. He noticed his servant enter the hall carrying a two handed tankard. He gestured at him irritably.

The minion hurried across the hall. His courage deserted him as soon as he entered the room and he began to tremble at his own audacity. Ripples formed on the surface of the murky brew in front of him. It smelled all right considering, but was not visually appealing. The mixture had adopted a brown colour topped with grey foam. Perhaps the few added drops of his own bodily fluids had been too much. He noticed the girl standing two paces behind Cassius and he drew strength from the sight of her. He dropped to one knee and offered the tankard with both hands outstretched above his head.

"About time." Hjovra eyed the brew suspiciously. "What's this?"

"Coffee Mix, my lord, as you requested." The minion kept his eyes averted.

Hjovra paused for a second and looked hard at his servant. Then he threw back his head and drank the contents in one long draught, his throat working in great spasms and his beard bobbing up and down as he swallowed. When he had finished he drew the back of his hand across his mouth and handed the tankard back to the minion.

"Good," he said. "Now bring me wine. Wine!"

"At once, Sire." The minion started to back away but could not resist adding "Perhaps, Lord Cassius would also..." but the look on Hjovra's face prevented him from continuing. He had hoped Cassius would send his minion to the kitchen at the same time so that they could steal a few moments alone. She winked at him as he passed and he smiled back.

A servant's life was hard and Hjovra was a particularly demanding master, which made it difficult to spend time with someone in another household. He hoped to cause Hjovra to tire of him and swop him or lend him to the kitchens. But it was a fine line between being considered a bad servant and a mere annoyance, to the extremes of punishment and the ultimate sanction, which was within his master's power.

A few days later he was fetching a coffee, no pick and mix this time - Hjovra had become more careful in his ordering - when the girl stepped out of a dim recess in the corridor. He almost dropped his tray.

She laughed and imitated his startled jump. She took his hand and guided him into the small alcove. "I'm Tes. What's your name?"

He was struck dumb for a moment. "You have your own name?"

"Of course. Don't you?" Cassius gives us all names. We are only allowed to use them among ourselves."

"Well I've never needed one before," he said defensively. "What are you doing here?"

"Waiting for you."

He let that pass; she was making him nervous.

"I will think of a name for you," she said and she kissed him quickly on the cheek. The alcove was very small and she was very close. The warm scent of her overpowered the smell of coffee and threatened to overpower him. He eased away from her.

"Sometimes I wish I was with Cassius; he seems much easier than Hjovra. I'm trying to get swopped."

"I've noticed," she laughed. "You'd like it. It's a good household we all get on together. I'm sure you would fit in."

"I've got to get away from Hjovra first."

"You will I'm sure."

"I'd better get back before this gets cold."

She walked beside him all the way back to the great hall.

As they entered there was a loud commotion at the Americas Table and a crowd began to form around it. A roar went up and a brief chant started.

"Intervene! Intervene! Intervene!"

"Looks like a major event," said Cassius to Hjovra. "Let's see what's going on."

Hjovra pushed his way to the front of the growing crowd. The Table showed a scene of devastation. He recognised the signs of a recent earthquake. Dazed people, dust, debris and rubble, collapsed or oddly angled buildings, gouged and mis-aligned streets. Nothing very extraordinary as earthquakes go. He had seen many, and had had a hand in a few. He watched as Nogrand delved an arm into the Table and sent an aftershock pulsing through the city causing more damage and mayhem. The crowd roared.

"So, what's the excitement?" said Hjovra.

"It's a bet," someone said. "Arcane has bet Nogrand he can create a love affair in the most exceptional circumstance."

"Ah! Now, that is more interesting."

Nogrand manipulated the view until he had found what he wanted.

"This will do nicely." He gestured to Arcane. "It's all yours."

Arcane studied the Table closely. It showed a woman of about thirty kneeling within the ruins of a house. She was no longer weeping but her face bore streaks where her tears had wiped away the dust. With hands, bloody and filthy from digging, she clutched another disembodied hand extending on the stalk of a forearm from the rubble. As they watched she released it and stood, head bowed, staring down at that final wave. Above, on the apex of a slope newly created by the wreckage of the building, a man watched her. He was older, by at least a decade, and he too was covered in dirt. The remains of a white shirt, now nearer the colour of his greying hair, flapped about him. He seemed uncertain of any course of action.

"A challenge indeed," said Arcane. The crowd murmured their agreement. Then he reached in and deftly dislodged a clump of masonry at the foot of the incline. The rubble became unstable and the slope moved bringing the man and a small avalanche of rocks and dust crashing down. He slid into the woman, knocking her off her feet.

Arcane closed his eyes and silently mouthed a few words. In the scene, the man said something to the woman. She half sat up and slapped the unfortunate survivor with all her strength. His head rocked back with the impact.

There was silence for a moment, and then the crowd erupted into laughter and roars of approval.

"Bravo!"

"Bravo! That's love no doubt about it."

"Swept off her feet."

"What did he say? What did he say?"

Nogrand and Arcane turned to look at Hjovra, seeking adjudication from the master. Hjovra stroked his beard for a moment.

"Inconclusive," he announced, "no winner. We will need to check again tomorrow." Both Nogrand and Arcane nodded in agreement and the crowd began to break up and return to work.

He was carrying a tankard of hot mead when Tes intercepted him again in the corridor.

"Hello, Jes," she said touching his face lightly.

He stopped "Is that my name?"

"Yes, like it?"

"Jes.... Jes." He tried it on. "Yes, it's like yours but slightly different."

"Lord Cassius has said that if you are dropped from Hjovra's service he will take you in."

"He knows I want to leave? You actually spoke to him, about me?"

"Things are different in our household," she said, "but you must do it soon before he loses interest. Today." She kissed him on the cheek and sped away along the corridor towards the hall. He followed on behind.

He - Jes, he kept repeating his new name inside his head - carried the mead over to his master, who was seated at the European Table with Azeos and Cassius.

"Look, what I've found," said Azeos peering into the Table. "I feel a need to intervene."

Hjovra leaned forward in his seat to see. A man was standing in a grubby kitchen, one hand holding a kettle, still plugged into the wall and the other a sheaf of papers that he was reading intently. "So?"

"He's been up all night to finish that story. He's going to have a coffee and then catch the first post. It's the last chance to beat the deadline. I think I'll do 'exercise in futility' but I could go for 'start of promising career'. What do you think?"

At that moment the minion staggered forward and fell, spilling the contents of the tankard across the Table. A wave of hot mead flowed onto Hjovra's lap. The Table sputtered and sparked. Hjovra leapt into the air with a curse.

In the Table, they all saw a jagged spear of light arc across from the socket to the man still holding the kettle. He flew backwards, arms flailing and papers flying making their own paler, slower arc. He bounced off the wall and slid to the floor. Faint wisps of smoke rose from his hair.

"Oops," said Azeos, "untimely death, I think." The Table flicked to another scene.

The minion slowly regained his feet. He did not look up. Everyone else looked at Hjovra.

Hjovra drew himself up to his full height and regarded his minion with distaste.

"Now, you die, you useless piece of ......"

"I'll swop him," said Cassius, laying a calming hand on Hjovra's shoulder.

"No! He's useless. He dies."

"I'll lock him up for a month and then retrain him. It was an accident I'm sure. No need for any bother. It's easier than making a new one."

Hjovra had calmed down a bit and saw the sense. "OK, I'll swop him for that one." He pointed at Tes, who let out a stifled little cry, but once again, Cassius came to their rescue.

"No, my friend. My best one for your worst is not a fair swop. Come for dinner tonight and you can choose one that is agreeable to us both. Now, I must get back to work."

Cassius headed back to the Africa Table. Tes nudged Jes and they followed a step behind, walking deliciously close together. They kept their heads down to hide their faces; servants should not be seen to be too happy.

Cassius on the other hand could not hide his grin. It had been a difficult challenge - to make an intervention beneath the nose of the master himself and Hjovra not to be aware of it. His long-standing wager with Arcane was well won.

Saigon Dream

I dream of Saigon, yes that city and that time. Those brilliant days, that buzzy atmosphere, where every moment of life seemed more important, more real, those moments that make for vivid memories, good for a lifetime. There you were alive every day in a sense that most people only experience at special events or catastrophes in their lives. The difference was that the whole city lived it day after day, lived to celebrate life while all around the carnage continued.

You could buy anything in Saigon, and I mean anything, a woman for an hour, a month or a year, or a boy if you wanted. Munitions, drugs, contraband - it was all for sale. Want a helicopter, a flame thrower, an M16 or even a tank - if you could afford it, it was available and most of it courtesy of the US government - anything could be signed off lost on a battlefield. I lived it briefly, for a day or two at a time, and these were memorable days.

But if you take away restraint, relax the rules, let justification replace justice, remove the fear of retribution or punishment then we must not expect bad memories to be any less vivid than the pleasurable good ones.

I was the second mate on a tanker. We were running out of Singapore into Saigon on a two-week round trip. Good money; we went on double pay as soon as we entered the war zone three miles off the coast of Vietnam.

A little scary, perhaps, but the extra money helped keep your mind off the eighteen thousand tons of avgas, aviation fuel, kerosene, helicopter juice, whatever you want to call it, that was our cargo, and the US army used a lot of it. Not forgetting the 200 tons of liquid propane carried in twin exposed tanks, mounted onto the foredeck, which gave an ungainly look to our ship. Some genius in head office had decided that we may as well supply domestic gas to the Yanks at the same time. He probably made director. It sounds crazy now, sailing all that jet fuel into a war zone with a gas tank mounted on top, but the pay was exceptional.

At Vung Tau pilot station at the mouth of the river, we would take aboard a squad of Marines from a heavily armed gunboat that would then escort us up the river to the massive tank farm at Nha Be where the US army stored their fuel. The river wound right up to the outskirts of the city of Saigon. Most of the way the land on either side of the river was dotted with hamlets and a patchwork of rice paddies interspersed at intervals with patches of dense forest that had not yet been cleared for cultivation or defoliated by the Americans. Some was still thick green jungle.

The patrol boat buzzed around us in great elongated circles, like a protective sheep dog, as we moved slowly up the river. Occasionally, they would send a burst of fire from their machine guns into the trees. At first, we thought they fired at the Viet Cong, but it was only at the whim of the gunners. Sometimes, the squad on the ship would sit on deck playing cards; rarely moving until they returned to the gunboat at the end of the trip. On other occasions, they would merrily fire their rifles into the jungle or drop grenades over the side to deter divers from attaching magnetic mines to the hull. A few years earlier another tanker had been sunk by a limpet mine.

The sergeant, in charge of the squad, was a huge black southerner with hands like paddles and a set of teeth to match that lit up his whole face when he smiled. Frank smiled a lot. He had an easy way with his men and would leave them on guard, while he downed a few beers with the bo'sun. Only occasionally would he bring them to heel if they became too unruly or fired their weapons too often.

We grew complacent. Each voyage was a little less scary. After all, we were a British merchant ship - just trading and not really part of the war.

It was Steven's first trip into Saigon. He had joined the ship on our last visit to Singapore. I remember him as if it were yesterday. He was brand new, just a boy really - a company cadet on his first trip to sea. I only really knew him for a week, although some parts of him I was to become more than intimate with. I remember his excitement as we approached the coast of Vietnam; he was not scared at all, he was nineteen and going to war.

We hove to at the mouth of the river to pick up the pilot, the jungle foliage adding teeth to the coastline on either side. Soon the patrol boat appeared and pulled alongside to deposit the squad of marines. It was a glorious tropical day with a gentle sea breeze that kept the worst of the heat at bay.

Steven and I were standing on the port bridge wing as we took a bend in the river. I had just explained to him how the helmsman steered the outer line to avoid the sand bar in the middle. We were heading back into the wheelhouse, so I could show him on the chart, when a single sniper round came out of the jungle and blew his head apart. He died instantly with no sound, except the sound a lifeless body makes as it crumbles to the deck. The hiss of clothes collapsing, the series of little bump noises as first his knees, hip, chest, shoulder and finally head hit the deck. Head. Head is face down on the neat bleached planking. It is opened. There is a hole in the back of it; there is red blood and pale brain and white bone. I am glad when the hole fills up with blood; I don't have to see inside anymore. I watch it overflow and start to stain the deck; it forms dark patterns in stark contrast to the sun whitened wood. I am vaguely aware of the crescendo of sound as the marines open fire and the gunboat carves a white arc into the river as it powers in towards the river bank and its heavy machine guns add a deeper sound to the noise of the gunfire. The squad empty their weapons uselessly into the jungle. Hundreds of rounds in exchange for one bullet, one single lump of lead and one forever empty head. Blood is splashed onto the wheelhouse door and on the deck and on me. My white uniform is covered in blood and brains. It is on me, on my face, in my hair, in my mouth. I am shaking. I am aware of Frank coming up behind me; he has seen it all before.

"Going home in a bag, son," he says.

The Captain is on the bridge now.

"No-one on my ship goes home in a bag, Sergeant. Now get your men calmed down, there's nothing to shoot at." Frank moves quickly away.

The Captain relieves me and I am sent below. I stand in the shower until I stop shaking. I wash away the gore. I cry a little, not for Steven but for myself. Disgust is my strongest emotion.

Frank found us that night at the Blue Moon, the bar that we always went to in Saigon. He looked strange; we had never seen him out of combat dress. He wore a bright Hawaiian shirt and shorts, the colours muted against his dark skin. We drank beer silently. There were five or six of us, maybe more. Some parts of that day are a little fuzzy while I remember other parts clearly.

Frank gets a beer and joins us; the glass is lost in his hand. We regard him sombrely. He surprises us; he is not here to commiserate.

"What you guys need is some payback."

We see his teeth but he is not smiling. It can be arranged. It started us talking. We are agreed by the end of the night to meet Frank on the next afternoon, for some crucial payback. We must bring a load of dollars. That's not much, for a life – for Steven's life. We don't care about the money, we are personally affronted.

We meet him outside the Blue Moon. It is hot and humid and our shirts stick to us making wet diamonds on our backs. There are only three of us. Some are on watch. Some perhaps have sensibly decided to stay away. We have collected the money easily. I remember thinking that we would probably go to the line and blaze away at the jungle or something similar. It was near the end and the war was not very far from Saigon. In another couple of years, it will be called Ho Chi Minh City. I feel brave enough to shoot at the jungle.

Frank drives the jeep to the outskirts of the city. We are waved through a heavily armed checkpoint. Not American, but South Vietnamese military police guard the area, known locally as 'White Mice' from their pristine helmets. They are universally feared and even Frank is deferential in their presence. We drive into a fortified compound and stop outside a low whitewashed building with more guards. They do not acknowledge us. Frank disappears inside taking the money with him. He returns after a few minutes and we follow another jeep filled with military police, down a dirt track behind the building.

"This is the Bullring," he says. "It's where the generals and the politicians come so they can tell their wives and their buddies back home just what war really is." He laughs shaking his head.

"They're prisoners of war, well mostly; sometimes they are just unlucky peasants. But it doesn't matter; the MPs kill them anyway. So if anyone asks, you are limey politicians, ok? There's a four-star general coming in tomorrow so they are only willing to give you one target." He must have seen something in our faces then because he quickly added.

"They tell me that this guy was a sniper caught in the delta area. There's even a small chance he is from the same unit that killed your boy. Either way it's good payback."

We arrive at the Bullring. It is a large dusty yard surrounded on three sides by a high wall. In the centre is a big wooden box with a bolted hatch on the side. A rope runs from the bolt back to the firing point where we are standing. It is an open area shaded by a low bamboo thatched roof. There are tables and chairs, steel weapons racks and a fridge filled with beer and Coke. Killing in comfort. The world has shifted under us and we have entered another level of Frank's world, a world where killing is for everyone.

Frank consults with the MPs and they disperse. Except for one, who is snicking ammunition rounds into magazines in a well-practised way on a long bench-like table. When he's finished he helps himself to a beer and then sits holding the end of the rope in one hand. Frank brings over three M16 assault rifles. He lays them down and loads the magazines into them one by one.

"It's simple, guys. The enemy is in the box. Pull the rope and he escapes. You shoot him. The MPs are on the outside of the wall, if he gets over they shoot him, but you don't get your money back."

He holds out rifles to my two shipmates, but they both refuse. They will only watch.

"Chickenshit limeys," mutters Frank. "What about you, you just want me to do it?"

I take a rifle from him.

"I've used a shotgun for clay pigeons before. Show me." I said.

He takes the gun from me. Works the bolt and hands it back.

"Safety here, single/auto here," he says, pointing to the small levers on the side of the gun. "Locked and loaded. You want rock and roll or single shot?"

"What's best?"

"Single shot," says Frank, "on full auto you'd shoot mostly sky. It'll still fire as fast as you can pull the trigger."

"Just flick the safety off and pull the trigger. I'll stay beside you." He picks up another rifle and quickly works the bolt to load the first round from the magazine.

"Yo! Shout 'Pull' when you're ready," he roars with laughter. "OK, safety off."

I click the switch and pull the gun into my shoulder. I resist the urge to shout 'Pull' like you do for clays. Frank waves at the MP and he tugs on the rope until the bolt opens. Nothing happens. The rifle becomes heavier and heavier as the seconds pass. I become conscious of the fact that I am preparing to kill a man. Part of me wants that experience, wants to live on that edge. There is an awesome power and beauty in that weapon. It is strange that the leading edge of human technology and ingenuity is always driven by the need for better ways to kill. Sweat runs into my eyes and I blink. Common sense begins to intrude and I realise I am incapable of killing another human being. I lower the rifle, I had not realised how tightly clamped in my grip it was. My arms ache with the release of tension. There is no one to shoot anyway.

The MP shouts something in Vietnamese. A pause, I am about to say something important. The hatch pushes back. A man crawls out on his knees. I am surprised that it is a real man. His arms are tied brutally high behind his back and he has difficulty getting to his feet. He is naked except for ragged black shorts. He looks confused, starts stumbling towards us, not running, not escaping. He calls something to us. The MP laughs and shouts abuse.

I can see the man has been severely beaten. One side of his face is puffed up and bloody the eye is closed and his body is marked and grazed. The blue of bruise and the black of dried blood compete for space on his torso. He is young but privation has etched the sinews and muscle and ribs starkly onto his body. His injuries make him ugly. I wipe the sweat off my forehead with the back of my wrist.

"Shoot....... SHOOT!"

I raise the rifle. Now it fits lightly into my hands, into my shoulder, into my cheek. Into my mind comes an image of my face seen through the telescopic sights of the sniper. The cross-hairs perfectly divide my head into quarters. The image moves and Steven's face replaces mine, mere millimetres of movement once separated my death from his. I see a vision of Steven's shattered head again. I blink and the man fills the sights in front of me. The rifle bucks in my hands. A spray of sweat and blood eject from the man's side, just above his hip. He spins away from us and screams as he falls; he twists in pain on the ground but then remains silent.

"Good," said Frank, let's go finish him. We stand over him. I look into the man's face. His eyes are clamped tightly shut, his face creased in pain and his chest is heaving but he struggles for control and then holds himself still. I see the side of his face that is unmarked; a single red bloody tear hangs at the corner of the eye. As I watch it lets go and runs down past his ear to the line of his jaw. It stops. His eye opens. He looks at me. He looks into my eyes.

"Too close," says Frank. He pulls me back a few paces. "Finish him now".

I pulled the trigger three times in quick succession. This time, I aimed carefully into the chest. I did not want to damage that face. The high powered rounds pass through his body as if it was not there. I am so close I feel the tremor of the earth through my feet as each round punches into the ground. They connect me to him. His torso is now a bloody pulpy mess but I do not wish to see anymore. I walk quickly back to the firing point. I put the rifle down and take a beer from the fridge. I remember the look on the faces of my two companions.

It was strangely easy to return to the world, to the ordered life of the ship. We three never spoke of it again. It was a month or more before he came for me the first time, but after that he came and still comes, thirty years later, in my dreams.

It always ends with the image of his unmarked face with a single bloody tear at the corner of his eye that waits and waits and waits before finally making that long, long journey down and - the part I dread the most - his one good eye opens to look at me.

Black

Oh, yes! These are the glory days, this is the renaissance, the enlightenment, and for me these are the good times. But I fear that they may not last. The unstoppable millwheel of taste will eventually grind us back to the dark. Back to the lost years, the endless searches, the dyeing and the mixing and the painting.

I live in fear.

I stockpile.

I stockpile endlessly for the drought that must come. I dread that time.

Take clothes, for example; Jeezus! In the seventies there were no black clothes. I bought white Levis and dyed them black, or at least a greyish colour. The stitching all stayed white – why was that? - I dyed them again. They got blacker but the stitching stayed white. I spent one long summer night painting the seams black with a felt tip pen, but I only finished one leg so I never wore them. I have a lot to thank punk for, although I hate to admit it. Punks and Goths, I still believe that their impact on the garment trade made black economically viable as a mainstream colour.

Sometimes, I remember that, when I admire my clothes stockpile. Black jeans in my size and the size above in case I put on weight and in the size below in case I get sick. The same three sizes in neat piles of trousers, tee shirts, shirts - well charcoal grey for shirts - socks and underwear. Black jocks for men were unheard of until the enlightenment. I also keep my collection of rarely worn black ties. It's impossible to wear a black tie without constantly being asked who has died. I compromised on black with a fine red stripe.

Do you know it wasn't until 1987 that you could order a car with black paint, order mind you and pay extra? It was not until the 90's that black became an option.

You get black toothbrushes now, but only recently. Mine is always black.

I used to buy hers -always red, mine always black so that she couldn't mix them up. She had a lousy memory; she could not recall things like that. But with black she could make no mistake. She's gone now. I think she overheard me once, describe her as 'Ok, but not my favourite colour'. It could have been the last straw or maybe not. But, at last I got to redecorate the house to my colours.

Remember when you could not buy black paint for love nor money. Well maybe gloss but certainly not emulsion. But as I said we live in the age of enlightenment.

Let me give you the tour. I'll start with the hall – white, pure brilliant white. Are you surprised? Pure white, from top to bottom and, on the largest wall, the one opposite the stairs a microdot of black. Invisible, but not insensible so that as you walk in the door you don't see the colour, you sense it. You feel the faintest shade of black. Ah, I know what you're thinking - white isn't really black, so it can't count. But it is. Black floods out from its deepest darkest shades through a thousand increments of light and then through another graduation of ever lighter greys until eventually white remains. White with a touch of dark, the microdot, is black. White is black, never the reverse.

Black is not a colour, it is not there in the spectrum, it is not primary, save by its absence and the fact that all other colours are absorbed into it. Black is the colour of emptiness, the colour of space and the colour inside.

White is black. You don't believe me. Then try this, try it at home, you'll be ok just go back if the red comes. You lie in bed at night in the dark, relax, except for your eyes. Open your eyes with the lids closed and look into the black. Keep looking, don't flinch, just bear the strain. Resist the urge to blink. Stare into the black. After a while you'll see the black get blacker, waves of black wash through, each time leaving a deeper shade behind. Are you scared now? See the black, it starts to smash into your skull in retina aching pulses. Black, blacker, blackest - stay away from the black-red. If you hold long enough, the black becomes so intense it cannot get darker, then suddenly, almost without warning the whiteout comes. Do that and tell me it's not true. White is black.

White in the hall. Light airy relaxing grey in the living room. Kitchen, shinier, silvery, utilitarian silver grey. Dining room darker, warmer, richer. We go upstairs now up above the white on the landing I've got strata of grey flowing up from the floor getting darker and darker until the band below the ceiling and the ceiling itself is iron-sea grey, battleship grey.

The bathroom, shiny like the kitchen but this time the shades come down from the iron grey ceiling continued from the hall in darker and darker bands. I used the same tin of grey paint as the ceiling but every band I added another careful measure of black emulsion, until by the time I reach the floor it is pure black and runs seamlessly into the black carpet. Now, that was hard to find. Hard to find a pure colour carpet without some fleck or speckle through it and unfortunately every spot of fluff or lint shows like a beacon so it's very hard to keep pristine. This carpet by the way goes through the whole house, except the guest room and the kitchen where there are black lino tiles - for some reason you've always been able to buy those - even in the seventies it was ok to have a black floor. The guest bedroom has, no you're wrong, cream walls, blue carpet and matching curtains, and the quilt cover has the only pattern in the house – an atrocious concoction of geometric shapes and bold brushed zigzags. It is a quilt of many colours but at least the zigs are black. The walls have nice pictures and it is here that I keep the little knickknacks and things that my mother sends me each year for my birthday and at Christmas - I keep two years' worth and as new ones come I throw the oldest away. Oh yes, she calls herself Mother now, with a capital M, now that it's easy. It's a very ordinary looking room and if I think I'm going to need it I always mess it up a bit as I've learned that to be too tidy is not a good thing. Is that more weird than being too neat? It's just that sometimes I really like to have that closeness with a female, you know. It's not so easy and these days it's rare that I can sustain a relationship long enough for any physical closeness to develop. And then of course when it does, well let's just say I don't live up to their expectations. I've noticed that women generally forgive a failure on the first occasion; in fact they almost seem to expect it, but they soon switch from fear of their own sexual unattractiveness to scorn. I don't mind too much as I mostly prefer my own company anyway.

That brings us to the main bedroom. No-one has ever seen inside that room, since I made it mine alone.

It is black. I could describe it but it would be boring and repetitive, save to say there is nothing in that room except the air that is not black. Even my presence in it reduces its purity.

Sometimes it scares me.

There is a flaw, I did not put it there, but there is a tiny opening scraped in the blackout paint of the window glass that each morning lets a single beam of light shine into the room, a tiny star of sunshine. It is this glorious beam that lets me start the day again, that gets me through one more time.

I will one day cover it, but not yet, not for a little while yet.

Larry's Future

Larry could tell the future. He had always been able to, although it was only in the last few years when he had finally accepted that middle age was fully upon him that he had started to analyse it. He had experimented with it more and more lately. In a way it was similar to quantum physics - the act of thinking about it was likely to change the result. A physics teacher had once told him that if you observe a photon using light to see with, the very act of seeing influences the state of the photon, and twenty years later he still did not understand it but the idea seemed to apply to predicting the future. Thinking about it altered the outcome.

He had to admit it hadn't done him much good so far. He wouldn't be sitting here in a too small uncomfortable seat waiting for take-off if it had. He'd be on a yacht somewhere baking in the Caribbean sun with a beautiful woman or two. He checked the time; damn the flight was already ten minutes late. There did not seem to be much happening. He looked down the length of the aisle to where the steward had his head stuck in the cockpit door. It was most probably a traffic delay; flights never seemed to leave on time from Heathrow these days. Larry always chose an aisle seat if he could, although he liked the view from the window especially at take-off and landing, but the claustrophobic element made him prefer the aisle. Worse of course was to be stuck in the centre seat on a busy flight - there are no rights to an armrest in that seat, or at least he had never figured out the rules of ownership.

The steward announced in that imperious and slightly peeved but polite voice, reserved worldwide solely for the use of flight attendants, that the delay was caused as one passenger was missing and they would wait a short time longer.

Larry sighed. He imagined the future as a vast fluid ocean ready to accept whatever was imposed on it by the ships and boats sailing on its waters. Thus individuals and events, whether natural or man-made, were like boats ploughing through the water. Their courses ever changing as decisions and events occur and interact. Each vessel's wake solidified behind it and became fixed into the past, but right up until that moment the future was unset and anything was possible. But as the future gets closer and closer the more unlikely it was that the course would alter the future. In short the nearer it is the easier it is to predict.

So it worked best when he didn't think about it and when it was closer. Sometimes a thought would pop into his head such as - I wonder what's happened to so and so or I still have not paid for this or that. Sure enough, as often as not, the next morning there would be a text from his friend or that missing bill would turn up in the post.

He was careful though - if a thought popped into his head he would trace back to see if there was any obvious linkage to recent events. Coincidence was not the same as prediction.

He was certain that if he could get near enough to the lottery in time he would have a much better chance of winning. Of course they knew this and that's why they closed the terminals a half hour before. He had carried out quite a few experiments and found that if he hung around until the very last minute, quickly scrawled the numbers down, without thinking of course, and rushed to the terminal just in time, then there was a much better chance of winning. He had often predicted three numbers and once four with this method.

It had its drawbacks though, not least the increasingly annoyed and less than helpful staff at the local corner shop. More than once he had to respond to the salesperson's comment.

'Sorry too late, terminal just closed'.

With a 'could not care less' look, a careful and slow ripping up of the form and a head held high exit.

The captain, his voice much more relaxed and re-assuring than the steward's, announced that there would be a further short delay. As they had been unable to find the passenger; they would now have to find his luggage in the hold and remove it before take-off. Well that explained why they had bothered to wait for the errant passenger. It shouldn't be too long, thought Larry, there won't be that much hold baggage on the shuttle flight.

Bigger, slower events could be predicted from a greater distance he had found. Relationships, for example. He could generally tell within the first few weeks of a new one roughly how long it would last and was invariably right to within a month or so. He had, although he did not officially count it, predicted the end of his marriage though it still came as quite a shock even if he had come to expect it.

Jobs and promotion were another slow predictable. He had correctly guessed his last two company changes and his most recent promotion. He had to admit there was no hint of the future on the job prospect front at the moment however hard he tried not to think about it.

The steward was making his way down the aisle checking seatbelts. The captain came on again to announce that they were ready for take-off and would do so as soon as the luggage had been removed. Larry could hear faint noises from beneath the floor as the ground crew searched through the hold.

Tony stood on the raised cargo platform at the hatch while Big Frank rummaged around in the baggage muttering the tag number under his breath.

"GL 148,......GL 148,......GL 148...., GL......., here it is, no...... no, Tony what's that number again?"

"GL 148" Tony sighed, reading it off the manifold list for the third time. "GL 148, R. Crane. You got it now." He heard Frank start to repeat the number under his breath again.

"I got it," called Big Frank, a few minutes later. "GL 148, it's big and it's heavy."

He picked it up awkwardly with both hands in the confined space and began lumbering back to the hatch with it. He stopped.

"It's ticking, Tony, it's ticking" he shouted. He dropped the bag and began scrambling towards the hatch.

Tony screamed at him. "Get it out! Get it out!" Then he backed out of the hatchway, leapt off the platform a full twenty foot drop and started across the tarmac in the direction of the terminal. He was limping badly.

Big Frank stared after him for a second or two, then turned back and quickly began hauling the case towards the hatch, all the while muttering under his breath.

"Shit, it's a bomb, shit it's a bomb shitits a bomb shititsa bomb shititsabomb shitsa bomb shitsabomb."

Directly overhead in the passenger cabin Larry, without thinking, foresaw the future.

"Shitsabomb. It's a fucking bomb!" he screamed.

His leap into the aisle was somewhat strangled by the seatbelt round his midriff. He fumbled for it and finally got it free. The steward was hurrying towards him; others were starting to become concerned, some were already standing. He pushed past and raced down the aisle with the steward in pursuit, still shouting wildly. The cockpit door opened as he approached it and the first officer appeared.

The officer and the steward tried to restrain him as he incoherently ranted on about a bomb, the sea and winning the lottery. Giving up any hope of understanding the railing passenger and putting together the unclaimed luggage and the talk of a bomb the first officer disappeared back into the cockpit and moments later the Captain announced he was evacuating the aircraft.

The doors burst open, the inflatable slides deployed and the passengers disembarked in a manner much more undignified then they had imagined. On the ground there was nothing unusual going on. A man in the bright florescent jacket of the ground crew was struggling back to the terminal carrying a huge suitcase clutched to his chest. In front of him was another, heading in the same direction but limping badly.

The first passengers to exit initially gathered around the bottom of the slides. Larry, as he had been right at the front of the aircraft was one of the first out, and was among them. Seeing the ground staff moving away from the plane the passengers as one started to follow and soon broke into a run in order to catch them up. A few barefooted or clutching high heels followed on at a slower pace.

Big Frank became aware of the crowd of passengers closing in behind him and tried to go faster but the huge suitcase weighed him down and he was barely managing a shambling walk. He turned to confront them searching for words to explain. At last he dropped the case and backed away with arms spread trying to be heard over the hubbub of the enquiring passengers.

Breathing hard, Larry plonked himself down on the case.

"This must be far enough, surely?"

Big Frank heard the ticking stop. He turned and ran, rapidly overtaking Tony. They exchanged a panic stricken stare for a moment as Big Frank ran alongside then with his huge thighs pumping wildly Frank sped on ahead.

The crowd of passengers, by now completely confused but with their initial panic beginning to lessen, watched them go and all began to gather closely around Larry who was still sitting on the suitcase. They looked at him as though somehow he had all the answers.

In the terminal Robert Crane woke up with a start and a sinking feeling in the pit of his stomach. He looked at his watch. Damn I missed my fight. Oversleeping had always been a big problem for Robert. The only thing that would wake him was a big old fashioned alarm clock that his mother had given him. It had a huge mechanical clanger on top.

Tear

when you cry alone
there is a small comfort
in the caress of a tear
warm on your own face

Book

I am aged
    and raggedy edged
I am a book
    old and well worn
My covers are marked
    and stained with
    splashes of spilled drinks
    greasy finger pads
    and cigarette burns
I am a book
    but you can open me
    page by page
    without too much effort
    and maybe find something
    worth knowing inside

Exocet

The ever present man
stalks, stomping through the ship
from rumbles in the bilges to raucous laughter in the bar
you can feel his presence and it's never very far
As she heels into another turn
the screaming sirens bring the men to stations
and some men light a cigarette like other men light a prayer
but no one looks behind them for fear that he'll be there
for the flashing battle lanterns brings his face too close to focus
and the inner silence sounds his words too close for comfort
As she starts another zigzag
and the blackout breaks the moon
then the circuits flash a warning
ten seconds, worth a damn
to the grinning, grinning face of the ever present man.

....lights the sea for miles around.

Untitled

my friend and lover comes but rarely
and when she comes
she comes in silence
and in the whisper of the wind
she gives not of herself
but of illusion

and when we lie in the deepest part of night
where sleep evades all thought
we set the rules of the game
that it still,
….saddens us to play

Four Minutes

I fell into the nightsky on a rumble of thunder and a dry lip.

Maybe not exactly thunder. I have a vague recollection of the fuselage rupturing in front of me as I am sucked towards it. Swept through it. A wing flailing above me. I must have been asleep, still am and probably drooling because I can feel the frightening wind freeze drying my bottom lip as I fall.

Falling into nothingness, extreme windnoise and cold. Brain engages; snap wide-awake. Time is passing extraordinarily slowly. Floating now, not falling and I have a vague hope that I have landed in something soft beside a bed, but the air is still shrieking past me. Terminal velocity I guess; the body only senses acceleration. I start to do the calculation in my head. I think the captain said thirty-six thousand feet last time I listened to the flight announcement. But I quickly realise by the time my limited capacity for mental arithmetic has coped with this problem I will probably have arrived. Forget it. Time slows down again. I concentrate on every second.

I decide to run through my life, it seems appropriate and it isn't starting to happen automatically. I take this as a good sign, maybe I will survive. Baby times - full of crap; childhood - nah skip it, so I jump quickly to my first teenage sexual encounter, but sex holds little interest at the moment. I must be falling in between those six minute male intervals. Forget it. Thinking speeds up time so I close it down again by focusing on every second.

I become aware that various objects, and bodies -

sometimes I hear a faint extended scream - as they pass, are overtaking me. This should not be so. Surely we should all be travelling at the same speed by now, terminal velocity. Still trying to elongate every second with one part of my brain I look around and realise that I have accidentally adopted the skydiver's position, belly down offering maximum resistance to the upcoming air. I am also spinning, rotating in a horizontal plane. I am spinning very fast. I know this, because the arcing fire of the doomed jetliner is now far below me and I am seeing it in stroboscopic effect as it snaps in and out of my vision as I rotate. For the first time in my life I want to be last, I don't mind being overtaken and I am damn sure I do not want to be first.

There is a faint and faraway sound of an explosion. The arc of fire has terminated. The plane must have been still under power to have already reached the ground. I resist the temptation to look at my watch to see how long I have been falling knowing that I have not looked before. Next time, I remind myself, to start counting as soon as the explosion occurs so I can do the calculation. I resist the urge to calculate, I also resist the urge to scream. I wish for a parachute. All these urges speed time up again and I close it down trying to tick off each microsecond as it occurs. I think for a moment it would be easier to countdown but I fight that thought.

I feel that I am flying like those lopsided autumn seeds you see spinning madly, carrying the next statistically rare generation. Not quite flying I remind myself, but spinning and falling.

The stroboscopic bonfire is getting noticeably nearer. In the gloom I notice something falling with me a few yards away. It is strobing in my vision as well, but at a much faster rate. At the risk of letting time loose I concentrate on it. It is an empty seat, spinning like me, flat against the upwind with the top tilted slightly down. I have a strong desire to sit in it and rest. I experiment with manoeuvring in the wind; it is tricky while rotating so fast. After a while I get the hang of it, pulsing an arm out from the rotor that I have become into the slipstream on the opposite side to the direction in which I want to go. I close the gap. Sometimes, I lose a beat and am pulled away again, but now I am getting more adept and mistakes are few. I am very close to the chair. It is a stunning shade of dark blue. How do we connect when we are both spinning? I contemplate the problem for a while, all the time counting off those microseconds. The fire is becoming brighter. Time, even slowed down time, eventually runs out. There is nothing to lose.

I choose the moment when our revolutions bring us head to head and I reach out and grab it. It is almost wrenched out of my hands as our spins interlock and clash. We buck and twist like wild horses as our two spins merge into one much larger and slower. We lose immense rotational speed and gain much down velocity. But I use my weight like a child on a swing, surging it back and forwards, increasing the momentum of the spin, our different weights help and we gain speed. We are one now, rotating about the offset centre of my arms clasped around the headrest. I know the seat wants to survive as well.

I sense the ground approaching, the burning wreckage looms large, we are spinning so fast now that the fire is a single band of multicoloured light that completely surrounds us; it is pulsing in synchronisation with our offset undulating spin. I marvel at its beauty. I love my own aliveness. I release my hold on time for I no longer care whether I live or die here. It is enough to have lived. I

let go of the seat and she spins away fracturing the night
with splinters of rainbow light as we become finally alone.

The Paedophile and the Tiger

Do you know what a tiger smells like? Do you think it smells of cat, of jungle, of power and the wild, perhaps of freedom? We know tigers, we see them every day. In boxes, on boxes, selling this or that, caged in the TV. On posters, in poems, in pictures, in paintings. Did you know that if a tiger stands just right, his stripes will match the bars of his cage and camouflage him? Tigers spend a lot of time pacing their cages trying to find that right place. We have made tigers small to fit into our televisions and we don't know their smell.

This one smells of dank, old carpets, rotting food and incontinence, but, oh yes, but, there is an underlying scent of savagery and danger, because I also smell blood. There is blood around its mouth - mine, there is blood on its flanks - tiger blood. I'm sitting awkwardly, one leg trapped beneath me and the other straight out in front. I have lifted its head, not as heavy as you may think, on to my lap; it is barely alive. It opened an amber eye as I moved it, but I can't tell if it sees me through that narrow, alien iris. Does it acknowledge me? A tiger lives and dies alone. I feel the link. I cradle its head in my arms, so that this tiger, my tiger, dies with me. It does not care. It stops me falling backwards. I want to remain upright. I stroke the fur on its head; it feels stiff, coarse, tough. This is real heavy duty outdoor fur, not the silky pampered coat of a cat. There is a scabby bald patch which looks sore. Not many people get to stroke the head of a tiger.

There is more than blood in the tiger's mouth. Shreds of flesh hang out from between its chipped and yellowed fangs. I have a huge hole in my inner thigh where it came from. I wonder what memories it recalled for you my tiger, tearing flesh, feeling living blood pulse into your mouth. I hope you have memories of the wild. I hope you were not born in captivity. Memories are better than never having lived at all.

They are coming now, fearfully, incongruously dressed in bullet proof vests and helmets, slowly, with rifles still raised. They come to police your death; they still fear you, fear that you will leap up and shoot back. Do tiger claws pierce bullet proof armour? I want them to take their time. I need this time. My blood is still pumping out of me. I can feel it. I am sitting in a pool of it. It is keeping the lower half of me warm, while the rest gets cooler; my heat draining away.

I hope God keeps his side of the bargain. It was only a small thing really, maybe just an excuse to give me some reason, any reason to do this. I could have stood and watched, run, gone for help, anything but step forward. So I asked God that if I did this, would he make sure that the newspapers, tomorrow, would not link that word with my name.

Paedophile. I never knew what that word meant; I had to look it up the first time I heard it. The dictionary definition wasn't much help. I tried some others, Bibliophile - lover of books, Anglophile, mediaophile, lovers of this and that. Paedophile - lover of children. Perhaps not so far from the truth. When I was a child the word didn't exist. I don't remember being scared. Any touch, any hug, any attention was better than none at all. I thought adults were always right. I wanted to please them.

I wanted to be noticed, be someone, be important, be loved.

Now, of course I know, I have been to enough sessions inside and out. I know they think it was wrong. They think I was damaged, think I was abused. They think that the theft of my childhood made me like this. But I am just me. I know now I was not better or stronger or more self-aware.

I was born in captivity and I have never known freedom. I hope you have, Tiger. My life has been spent in cages; council homes or prisons or in fear of them. I have only been out a few weeks this time and I had decided it was better to live without love than to risk it again. I have been strong until today.

It was only minutes ago that I walked around the corner into the main street, invisible as usual. The street was deserted and unusually quiet for a Saturday morning. There had been some sort of traffic accident, but it did not explain the lack of people. I saw that a large truck had come off the road and was canted at an odd angle downwards through the railings onto the pavement. The shops and walkways there are set slightly below street level. Another truck had crashed into it and smashed open the rear doors. Both trucks bore the legend 'The Great State Circus' in fancy but faded script. I still didn't understand why there were no people.

A fat ugly little man waved frantically at me from behind the first truck and finally I saw what my eyes had already registered. A tiger in the road; a tiger in the high street. It seemed exotically out of place, yet at the same time its common image invoked familiarity. At first I thought someone was filming before I made the connection with the trucks. I had not known that there were any circuses left. The tiger was standing motionless in the middle of the road, beside an overturned supermarket trolley. Food packages, bottles and tins were scattered all around and, in the midst of this lesser wreckage, a small child lay face down, hair stained with blood. The child whimpered. The tiger seemed tired, uncertain. It had to act like a tiger even just after a road accident. Humans would lie down and let others take over. I started to back away, back to my corner but it looked at me and growled. I froze.

Its attention was drawn back to the child as it whimpered again. The tiger put its paw on the child's back for a moment and then, hooking a claw into the wool of the little blue jumper, turned it over. The child was silenced. I heard from some safer place the scream only a mother can give.

It was then that I made my bargain with God. I searched my pockets for a suitable weapon to fight a tiger. There wasn't much to work with. I found a topless ball-point with a chewed end. I could kill the tiger by stabbing the pen through its eye into its brain. I waited; maybe I would not be needed.

In the distance I heard the sirens. The volume increased as they got closer. The tiger roared back once, in defiance, and then again, louder and deeper. The child rolled onto its front and began to crawl away. Once again the tiger put its paw on the child's back and again I heard the despair of the mother.

I stepped forward, clutching my pen like a dagger. I shouted. I ordered the tiger to look this way, to leave the child alone. I am no longer invisible. People see me. The tiger sees me. Suddenly it seemed huge. I had thought it was further away. I thought there would be more time. It came at me, slowly at first, then in a blinding burst of speed. It leapt, raking my back as I tried to twist away. It landed, skidding on its claws and turned to face me and for one long moment we looked at each other. My back tingled and grew warm. I saw the mother carry the child to safety. My job was already done and I had done nothing, nothing except give up everything. The tiger charged again with awesome speed. I screamed. I can still feel its teeth, the pressure of its jaws, the ripping and tearing of cloth and flesh. I screamed. I heard the shots long after the bullets had already removed its magnificence.

The weak winter sun glints off something lying in the street and I realise that it is the mighty and forgotten pen. Finally they reach me and lift the tiger away, exposing the red puddle of my heat in which I sit and we are separated. A single shot marks the tiger's place. The ambulance men hurry over to me. They are too late. My vision is starting to blur but I see the mother approaching, cradling the child in her arms. I am fearful, at first, in case she knows about me and I am helpless, but then I remember that this mother cannot know me, cannot hate me. Tears are streaming down her face and she is mouthing words I can no longer hear. She kneels beside me and the tiny child reaches arms around my neck and bestows on my forehead, a kiss, chaste and pure.

(Auaarrgg! Fuckinhumans......A loud bang and the cage has suddenly tilted. I pad-slap claws into the filthy wooden floor to stop myself sliding down. There is a lot of shouting, Pigbelly is scrambling around outside, looking worried. I growl. It looks into the cage. It smells more bitter than usual and soon scurries away. One day Pigbelly I'll kill you. One day when these forever bars are gone.

Pigbelly thinks it is my master yet it fears me so much it stinks. Most times when it beats me or prods me through the bars I ignore it, so that it gets more careless. Then when Pigbelly least expects it I attack. Once or twice I've got real close to opening Pigbelly. When that happens it goes white, smells worse than usual and leaves me alone for many days. I am wondering why it smells like that now.

Then, I finally take in what my eyes have been seeing. There is a gap, there is a hole where no bars cover and it is large enough for me. I am on my way. Home.

Outside! Outside it is very confusing. Not open but at least the sky is not covered over. I hear fuckinhumans shouting and screaming but I cannot see them. I don't know which way to go. There is not much choice; a lot of the ways are blocked. I stop and sense a moment. I stand still. I try to smell the jungle but there is nothing except the overpowering stench of fuckinhumans and their things.

One of them walks into the clearing from one of the open ways. Its smell is unknown to me. I growl a warning not to come near and it starts to back away. It has some sense. I think I will go that way. Then a mewling noise attracts my attention. It is a fuckinhuman cub, hurt and abandoned. I put a comforting paw on its back hoping it will shut up and allow me time to think. It goes quiet.

Some fuckinhuman screams from somewhere I can't see. I hook a claw gently into the cub and flip it over. I think it will be OK. Maybe Pigbelly has attacked it. These fuckinhumans are capable of anything.

Now I hear wailing from fuckinhuman things, they approach. I roar back my answer. It feels good; it's been a long time since I roared. I do it again. It is one of my best; you need to be outside to really roar. It is full of power. If there are others near they will know that I am free. The cub turns over and starts to crawl away. I put a paw on it to stop it.

The strange fuckinhuman shouts at me and starts to attack. That's fine. I am free. I can walk, I can run, I can hunt, I can kill. It feels good. It turns away as I leap but I slash my claws down its back to weaken it. I had forgotten that full feeling as your claws clog up with fur and flesh. I land neatly and turn to face it. I am panting and tired but alive. I pause for a moment to relish the kill. It stands turning to face me. It is fearless like me. I have some respect for a few fuckinhumans. This is one of them. Foe and food. I see the cub's mother finally come to its rescue; I wonder what took her so long.

I attack, I leap. It is more powerful than I thought. Somehow it hits me with two massive blows that bring me to my knees but I carry on, sinking my jaws deep into its flesh. Pulling away I feel my mouth fill with blood, fill with life. I bring it down but I am strangely weary, I cannot be bothered to continue the kill. I lie still, feeling the strength from my limbs ebb away. I must go home.

The fuckinhuman lifts my head gently onto itself and strokes my fur. I allow it; not many would.

I feel a link with it. Now, over the warm stench of fuckinhuman blood, I can faintly smell the jungle. Now, I know if I could stand and sense the air I would know the way. I am going home.)

Flamenco Dancer

Ah…..but wait, I see a skirt, orange, bright orange with a wide frilled hem, which slashes up from one ankle to the opposite hip. It is wide and full volume and gives the impression of flowing movement even when at rest. I see a shoe, black with silver straps and flashes and square wide Cuban heels. Above I see her ankle, a muscular but definitely feminine ankle. Stitched to the hem of the skirt here at the ankle is a single tiny silver bell. It is so small that I wonder how anyone would ever hear its sound. Then I realise that as she waits for the absolute silence that she demands before she will start her dance; she will swish that side of her skirt just once and her lover will hear that tiny silver chime, because only he listens for it and then he knows, as always, that she dances not for the audience but for him.

Above the skirt the bodice is black, panelled and studded with silver, and arches up into a high collar that supports her slender neck. I see only her profile as she waits, poised, one arm straight up with wrist flexed and finger extended, the other bent to her waist. Her head is turned to the side - she will snap it round to the front when the dance begins. Her eyes are dark, almost black and deep enough to drown in should any other man dare. Her face is starkly pale against her midnight hair which is winched up into an uncomfortably tight bun. She does not wear a flower here but, instead two long, thin, silver barrettes with sharpened points, more reminiscent of geisha than flamenco, are pushed through in parallel. These were once more useful in her younger, wilder days when she danced the port bars of Caracas and Aruba and Curacao, and many a sailor's wandering hand still bears the puncture scar.

When Water Burns

They had the hatch manually locked and a jump lead, fashioned from a piece of uninsulated metal, across the control circuit so it could not be opened remotely. Tio sat leaning up against the hatch anyway just to be on the safe side, with his legs drawn up in front of him. He looked drawn and ill, as did his companion who was crammed into the two man emergency escape pod with him. Two narrow acceleration couches took up almost all available space. Rold lay in one of them, trying to get the images of the heaps of unidentifiable desiccated body parts they had encountered on the way to the pod out of his mind. They littered the once pristine passage ways. He rubbed absently at a small brand high up on his right cheekbone. It consisted of a triangle within a small circle both dissected by three parallel lines. It was a habit when he was nervous and lately it had been rubbed a lot. They were both unshaven, unwashed and wore filthy badly marked coveralls that had probably once been a shade of company blue. The shoulder patches marked them as Techs.

The pod had been ransacked. There were no intact ration packs or fluid bulbs, some were empty and had formed part of the rubbish on the floor but most had just gone. All the storage bins had been emptied. They had quickly searched through the debris when they had entered an hour or so ago but found nothing drinkable. Rold had tidied everything up into one of the bins, while Tio had arched his head back and squeezed every empty fluid bulb over his mouth but there was not a drop of water in any of them. They still had several hours to wait. Tio held a cup half filled with water and covered with film cradled carefully in his lap. He took a sip and then offered it to Rold.

Rold was slightly taller than Tio, but both had the tall thin spacer build from a life spent in low gravity. Tio had a family brand as well although his was different. The brands marked them as belonging to Traveller families, who lived their lives in space and crewed most of the long haul ships. Often the main part of an extended family was tied to one ship. When a child reached adulthood they could choose to stay on the ship and perhaps mate with a member of another family or sign up to another ship or of course go groundside. The time dilation effects of travelling faster than light meant that time was relative to you and those you travelled with. Leave the ship and you were on a different timeline, whether planetbound, on an orbital station or on another ship. So the family brands as well as helping in identification on the ships themselves were also a handy aid to prevent in-breeding in the bars and nightlife of the orbital stations, where that handsome or beautiful spacer may well be a very close relative. Age was relative and the stories of spacers mating with or even falling in love with their children or their parents always made good fiction.

One hundred and thirty five shipdays since the fire; one hundred and thirty five long dry days. Rold had been off duty and asleep when the fusion generator blew. Tio was on duty but not in the main engine compartment so survived the initial blast which killed all those who were.

There were around two thousand people on the ship – mostly passengers and their families, although most were travelling for work or relocation not for pleasure – only the highest echelons travelled for pleasure and in order to remain at the same relative age, their whole families had to travel with them. Rold reckoned that most of the passengers did not know what had actually happened.

When the fusion generator blew, the automatic safety programmes immediately shutdown all the generators, and the main engines that they powered, and flipped the ship into sub light normal space. Even these computer controlled sequences were not quick enough to stop a beam of ultra-high temperature plasma rupture the already damaged containment and punch through the bulkhead of the main engine space and then through the much thinner skin of domestic water storage tank Number 2, which nestled up to the bulkhead in the auxiliary plant room next door. This contained the machinery and recycling systems that provided air, water, power, heating and waste services to the passengers and crew. Here almost everything was recycled back into the ecosystem of the ship. Number 2 water tank contained 60 tonnes of slightly cooled, pressurised, and pure domestic drinking and washing water, of course it had all been recycled countless times but the makers of the recycling plant guaranteed that you would never taste the difference. On the other side of the ship Number 1 tank contained a similar volume.

Number 2 tank responded to being punctured by releasing a fine spray of water back out through the puncture wound onto the metal of the bulkhead. As this metal was at several thousand degrees centigrade the water, already warmed by absorbing the heat of the plasma burst, quickly became steam, then superheated steam, then supercritical and then in the space of only a few seconds began to disassociate into oxygen and hydrogen. The hydrogen ignited and burned brightly in the plentiful oxygen. The fire became self-sustaining requiring nothing other than water to burn and there were tonnes of that. This flame was not the normal orange and red but blue shading to intense white at the core. The temperature began to ramp up immediately and the compartment bulkhead started to melt.

The fire set off the detectors in both compartments and the automated systems again reacted the way they had been designed. Both compartments flooded with fire suppressant gas designed to suffocate the flames by removing the contact with the oxygen. This succeeded in putting out the secondary fires that were beginning to take hold, but made no difference to the water fire that continued unabated. Evacuation alarms sounded, to only the dead, in the main engine compartment and emergency breathing refuges opened. After a brief period, all internal hatches and refuges sealed and the vents opened to the vacuum of space. This last resort of expelling all the air from a compartment would of course have extinguished any fire. Any fire except this one.

Even in the vacuum of space water burns.

Three minutes later the vents closed. The fire still burned and the temperature of the bulkheads around the auxiliary compartment began to climb again spreading in all directions from the white hot flame.

The crew were soon organised into fire and damage control teams and were faced with small outbreaks where any combustible material came in contact with the searing heat of the bulkheads. On all sides and above and below, as the area of intense heat spread from the main flame, more fires started. Where they could they sealed rooms and allowed the fire suppressing gas to control the fires. But in the passageways and corridors the only way to control the spread was to cool the metal of the bulkhead and try to prevent the heat spreading any further. The firefighting capabilities of the ship depended on the highly effective suppressant gas system but this was useless for cooling so the crew resorted to the age old method of forming human chains to throw buckets of water onto red hot metal or used any type of hose to project water onto the affected parts of the bulkhead from any available water outlet.

Both domestic water tanks drained together. The one feeding the water fire and the other supplying the huge amounts of water used to dissipate the heat. All the ships water supply slowly drained away. This should not have mattered as the ship was a closed ecosystem so all the water could be recovered and recycled whether from the drains and sumps or sucked back out of the atmosphere.

The ship was awash with water. It was ankle deep in places from the primitive firefighting and the atmosphere was thick with moisture and steam as well as smoke. Steam not only created from the water which boiled off the hot metal but also unburnt oxygen and hydrogen that had escaped the flame soon recombined into water in the atmosphere. The walls, decks and ceilings throughout the ship were coated in condensation and in some places where a mass of moisture laden air rolled down into a cooler section of the ship brief rain showers occurred.

Eventually the water fire died when there was simply no more water to burn. Rold had been deep in the thick of firefighting and was already suited up against the smoke and steam when the Bridge ordered anyone who was not already in sealed cabins or refuges into suits or emergency hoods. Both water tanks were empty – almost all the ships water was sloshing about the ship. All the fire suppressant gas had long been exhausted but there were still uncontrollable fires raging in a dozen different places.

The Bridge vented the air from the whole ship and waited long minutes for the cold of space to drop the temperature throughout the vessel. Rold wrapped his arms around a stanchion, as at first the air whistled past him but then diminished to quietness as the internal space of the ship equalised with the vacuum outside. He was grateful for the rest as he waited out those long minutes.

All the fires extinguished immediately as soon as the air was removed. Out into space went the water, sucked into the vacuum from the decks and the drains. The steam and smoke disappeared with the air in an instant and the condensation sublimated from every surface a few seconds later.

There is no water in space. There was barely any water left in the closed environment of the ship with one thousand eight hundred and eighty three survivors on board.

It took several hours for the air to be replenished from the high pressure gas tanks that contained the reserve, but once the crew and passengers were able to get out of their protective suits or emerge from refuges a sense of relief at having survived began to pervade the ship.

A semblance of normality returned for several shipdays. At first people gathered in the public spaces and canteens and despite the loss of life people who were grateful to be alive enjoyed a new found camaraderie that had not been present before. People pitched in together, both passengers and crew, as there was plenty of work to be done in clearing up and carrying out repairs.

It did not last long.

What dregs of water remained in the tanks and the recycler was gone in a couple of shipdays. The recycler continued to work for a while as it was able to extract a little moisture from the air and the waste and sewage systems. The hoarding started almost immediately by those who began to see the problem sooner than the others and less and less was recycled until not enough water was in the system to keep the plant operating. Then people no longer gathered but retreated to cabins or formed small groups. Fifteen shipdays after the fire the Bridge sealed itself off from the rest of the ship with most of the surviving officers and high echelon passengers and their families barricaded within.

Rold and Tio had teamed up early on when they realised that discipline was not going to restrain eighteen hundred or so very thirsty people. Being Tech they had access to parts of the ship that others did not and had become part of a group of Techs and Sub Techs hiding out within the machinery sections of the ship and draining pipe systems for water. Bends and surge vessels contained a surprising amount. Cooling systems were also a resource although the water had to be boiled and distilled to remove corrosion prevention chemicals. The Techs made up various small heater/distillers for this in the workshops. An industry sprang up selling them to passengers for water, non-dry food or sexual favours. As the amount of water rapidly diminished the distillers came in very useful for producing drinking water from anything - waste, urine, or any dirty water.

Eventually almost all of the total water content of the ecosystem of the ship was contained within the bodies of its people.

The killing started. At first merely for the blood but this did not last long as too much fluid was wasted and blood did not make a good thirst quencher – too salty. Soon extracting water from the bodies of the dead became the prime means of survival and the distillers were converted to cope with extracting the water from sliced or mashed up flesh. At first groups hunted individuals, but large groups needed many individuals to render down to water so soon larger groups attacked smaller ones resulting in pitched battles and then many days of quiet and hard work as the survivors rendered down the flesh to extract the water from the dead.

Rold and Tio left their group before things got to that stage when they realised that there was not enough water being recovered from the systems to supply the whole group. Some had taken to hunting passengers and they knew it was only a matter of time before the group turned on itself.

Rold and Tio hid out in the sewage recycler for a while and then in the ventilation ducts because as the killing became more common, more moisture entered the atmosphere and they had found places in the shafts and ducts where it was possible to lick condensation from the walls. They had a contact on the Bridge. They waited.

The Bridge, in ship's slang referred not only to a location but also to the combination of several AI's linked and controlled by a human brain which commanded the ship. After catastrophes inflicted on several worlds by rogue AI's they were almost universally banned except when working in synergy with a human. And these AI/human combinations were only used when absolutely essential such as navigating an interstellar ship at superlight speed.

Tio bought the pod's screen online and accessed the Universal Encyclopaedia. He was looking for information on the approaching star system. They knew about it because Tio had contact with an extended family member, Flave, also a Tech, who had been on the Bridge when it was sealed off. She had kept in touch through the ship's maintenance system by typing messages in the log. The officers and high echelon passengers had removed most of the crew from the Bridge deck before isolating it although for obvious reasons they had kept a handful of Techs. The Bridge had a shuttle dock attached to it which had a small recycler. So the Bridge had a limited supply of water that it was not for sharing with the main part of the ship.

They knew from Flave that, because of the initial fusion generator explosion and the resulting fire damage, the ship did not have enough power capacity to restart the superlight drive so they were condemned to cruise at sub light speed. The best estimate for reaching a civilised world capable of repairing the drive was about eight shipyears. There was of course a faint chance that they would meet another ship before then that could resupply them with water.

They had also learned that the ship was fast approaching a system where the third planet was habitable. There was no way the ship could decelerate in time and even if it could there was nowhere for it to dock - but the escape pods and the shuttle could reach the planet. The Bridge had decided that this was the best survival option and intended to abandon the bulk of the remaining people on the ship and concentrate on saving itself, the officers and the high echelon people.

The bio module that contained the AI/human had already had itself installed in the shuttle and Flave reckoned she could also wangle herself a seat on it. As there were more people than the shuttle and the escape pods located on the Bridge could accommodate the remainder would foray out just before launch and use pods in the main body of the ship.

This is why Rold and Tio had claimed theirs well in advance. Tio punched in the system number and then the planet id. They both read the screen.

"It's pretty, and humanoid which is good," said Rold. "But it's only Level 2 - barely above savages."

"And we're 5 – what does that tell you about savages?" responded Tio, who carried on flicking through the text. "I don't understand why there's been no contact. Ah, yes here. They won't make it through the Energy Barrier - well 93% chance of failing. No contact is normal procedure until a planet is successfully through."

"Barrier?" asked Rold.

"Yeh, not many make it through. Advanced civilisation takes a lot of energy not many planets make it without either killing each other off fighting over resources, polluting their planet so much it becomes uninhabitable or merely depleting all the reserves without becoming advanced enough to develop the higher energy sources."

"I've never heard that before," said Rold.

"It's why there are millions of planets but only a few hundred with civilisations above Level 3," replied Tio. "This one is overheating and has about a hundred solar years left. After that it will be water and not much else."

"Water! Sounds good to me. Plenty of time for a rescue ship as well."

"We should strap in, it's not long to go and the launch will be automatic." Tio started bringing the pod's systems online.

Flave had told them that the Bridge had chosen a landing zone in a country called China. It had put together a rudimentary language course and an information pack, based on transmissions it had monitored, that should be enough to help facilitate any initial contact after landing. Flave had passed it to them and they had both spent a little time on the language. China had been chosen by the Bridge as the largest, peaceable and stable country with one of the most widely used languages. Looking at the grainy pictures Rold was not so sure they would fit in well enough to go unnoticed and the Bridge's recent record on decision making did not inspire any confidence.

It was only about fifteen minutes to launch when they heard movement outside. The extra Bridge personnel must be making their way to the pods in the main body of the ship. Rold looked at the circuit jump lead to make sure it was still in place. All went quiet again.

"I hope there's enough spare pods without this one," whispered Tio.

A short time later they heard muffled shouts, screams and the sound of fighting.

"They've run into some 'distillers' then," said Rold grimly, rubbing at his cheekbone.

They both jumped as something heavy and metallic started battering at the hatch.

"Shit," cried Tio. "If they do too much damage it may not launch".

Rold flicked off the safety cover from the manual override.

"There's only a few minutes left - let's go now."

"Wait, wait! Or we won't hit the landing zone with the others," cried Tio. Outside the banging got louder. "Oh shit, you're right. Go! Launch!"

Rold hit the red button of the manual launch override with his fist. They heard the outer hull hatch blow off and then were pressed back into the couches as they accelerated down the tube and popped out into space. Almost immediately the pod started manoeuvring with its thrusters aiming at the planet, which was still a faint circle in the distance.

As the pod rotated Rold could see through a small viewport above his head several other pods eject from the main body of the ship. As it rotated further the upper part of the ship swung into view and he was heartened to see the sleek lines of the shuttle detach and start to move away together with another batch of pods. As he watched a sudden silent flash of flame consumed the shuttle and it was gone in an instant except for a few large pieces tumbling away from the bulk of the ship. Shocked – his first thoughts were for Flave, he hoped she had failed to get a seat in the shuttle and had been in one of the pods. He decided not to tell Tio until they had landed.

An hour later the planet, blue and white, filled the screen and the viewport and they were pressed into the acceleration couches as the pod started skimming the atmosphere to lose speed. Rold caught his breath as the pressure forced him into the couch.

"Will we make the landing zone?" he said.

"Doubt it but as long as there's water who cares," said Tio and hesitantly added, "*Hay war shuey.*"

"Uh….please may I have some water."

"Spot on," said Tio, "it's the only phrase I remember. Not going to be much use though, it's more likely we land on the other side of the planet."

Heat shields slid over the ports, closing off their view of the blue planet, as the pod dipped ever deeper into the atmosphere and the shriek of friction and the violent vibration made any further speech impossible.

"*Knee how*", whispered Rold to himself, hello world.

Chinese Restaurant

Who me? Late?

Jeez boss. Tables five, seven, nine, four and two. You're kidding right. Time you got some more help in. And help out with drinks - don't I always.

2
Rare single.

9
Fat red dress shovelling rice onto already top heavy plate. Spiky haired young old husband waving prawn cracker like laser pointer. Probably lucky to get one, hanging on to it before it can disappear down red dress. She grabbing the almost empty basket nearer. Proves point.

"Hey! Hey, miss! Er, you're no Chinese. We ordered fried rice nae boiled rice. She didnae notice before she started."

"Sorry, Ah only put a wee bit on. I wisnae sure of the difference"

"I ordered fried, definit-etly, did I no May?"

"Aye, yer did, Ah remember yer ordered fried."

"You'll no be charging me for both."

Perhaps madam would care to try our special low calorie rice.

4
Well-dressed curly haired woman. Man not so well dressed, not so curly haired, may once have been. Women

always talk more in restaurants or maybe just over food. Oh oh, they've been on that course 'Making the most of the movies'.

"His last film was far better. He's lost some sense of direction. But I thought she was perfect for the part. You wouldn't have known she was American, well there was that one scene where her accent slipped a little, and her hair was absolutely right for the forties."

"His last movie was a completely different genre, surely. You can't compare it. I don't think we're ready yet could you give us another minute. Thanks. And can I have a bottle of Becks please. Thanks."

"And a gin and tonic for me, please."

Correction Film appreciation for beginners.

7

Angry and Angrier. Interesting, oh don't stop now.

"I'm telling you for the last time I won't…..Ah! could we have another coffee please."

5

Family outing. Look we are the perfect family - we even take our teenagers out to dinner. Going grey beard with two very small food particles, not rice, too dark. Girl older, funny colour hair. Read instructions next time. Plump boy, greasy hair, greasy chin, computer eyes, making war manoeuvres with grains of rice on tabletop. Maggots defending the gravy stain. Wasted salt ramparts. Solid mum, not saying much, faint clothes, faint moustache. Father has all the words.

".... but Dad I really want to drop it. I don't understand any of it, it's all formulas and equations."

"Formulae. There is always an easy way to remember them. Even Einstein's E equals MC squared can be simplified to the faster you go the heavier you get."

"What?"

"Well roughly. Yes we've all finished. Tod you have finished haven't you? Thanks."

"Thanks."

"Yes, we'll see the dessert menu. Thanks"

2

Silent. Single.

Well nice nod, but you could have said something. I'll try not to spill your coffee in that tight-jeaned lap.

7

Sneak up with coffee. Unobtrusive. I'm not listening, honest.

"You bastard!"

"That's just like you, turn…Thanks."

"Um, thanks."

Pish.

9

No chopsticks here. Too slow. Perhaps the lady would like a bigger spoon.

"Ah! fried rice, 'bout time. This is, instead of, mind. We didnae order the boiled rice y'know. Are you awright now May?

"Aye, but there's no much chicken in this sweet and sour. It's all sweet and no much sour and I'm no sure what these green thingies are."

"Will I send it back, then?"

"Naw it's awright. It's hot enough."

4

"Thanks, I'm the duck. Have you read the book?"

"Yes, but it's years ago now. I think they've changed the ending. That's mine thanks. I think I'll read it again."

"Books are always better than the movie."

".. except in porno – you always say that."

"I was going to say Star Wars actually. That's fine thanks."

"Thank you."

5

Major as salt, the rice maggots are overwhelmed. The mother's a mute she won't even order her own food.

"Tod! Will you stop playing with the condiments!"

"condi – whats?"

"You haven't given it a chance, give it another term, university isn't like school you know."

"I hate the course I'm doing."

"Dad, Dad I want a toffee apple. We have to order now."

"Tod, stop interrupting your sister. Thanks we'll have two lychees and a toffee apple. What about you?"

"Nothing, thanks."

Perhaps sir would like a comb for his beard and madam perhaps a depilatory cream with her lychees.

2

Silent. Single. Sexy. I'll forgive you if you at least smile this time.

Pish.

7

"…. and crying is effing blackmail."

"Could you bring me another glass of wine please?"

"We've just had coffee."

"Well, if you can't stretch to it, I'll not bother."

"Glass of white and a whiskey please."

Right. I'm just going to fill it in then. He's been razzing your best friend, no, make that your best friend's mother and he expects you to forgive him and let him go to the football with his pals. Get wise and walk you silly cow. He's not worth it.

9

"…pizza on the way hame. Chinese just goes right through you."

"Pint o'heavy an' pint o'lager please miss. And can you bring the bill please."

Jeez mister, I hope you're on the top bunk tonight.

7

She's going, she's going. Left the wine. Good for you. He's waving for the bill, scribbling in the air with an imaginary pen.

Sorry sir, I didn't see that.

2

Nice eyes. No more coffee. Bill as well then. Go on smile you bastard. You're not very good at signals. If I wag my bum any harder my tights will fall down.

4

"Yes finished thanks, very good. I enjoyed it."

"Are you having a sweet, dear."

"Chinese tea, please."

"For two. Thanks."

"The characters weren't…. well, they just weren't solid enough. That's why the end didn't make me cry."

Pish.

7

Going. Going. Money on table. Oh good, not waiting for change.

9

Red dress and spiky now. Negotiate your gut around the table while I negotiate the bill dear.

"Er, miss. We thought the prawn crackers were free. No, oh well. Here you are. That's exact I think."

"Jim, Jim yer need tae leave a wee tip."

"Aye well, here's a pund."

5

Still eating, playing, sulking and silent.

2

"Here's your bill sir. I hope you enjoyed your meal. Look, that's weird - the numbers in your bill, seventeen sixty-eight, are all in my phone number. I've written it out in full on the back. Don't you think it must mean something."

Confused, but yes, a wee smile. Too late mister that's the number for the sauna next door.

Have fun and goodnight.

The Tramp

Lucy spent most of the summer days in the park. She lived just across from it. The park was a large square surrounded by streets of houses on all sides. Today she wasn't doing much more than avoiding her older brother who had a nasty tendency to bully her at every opportunity. She passed the tramp sitting on one of the benches with his head bowed. She had seen him before and knew he lived behind the public toilets at the far end of the park. Behind the low brick building was a clump of rhododendrons, small trees and piles of soil, gravel and grass cuttings. This place produced a mixture of rich earthy smells which competed with and sometimes complemented the more acrid aromas emerging from the building.

She stopped. On the path in front of her lay a small bird, oddly out of shape; less round than it should be and with one wing extended and eyes open. She was not sure whether it was alive or dead. She cupped it into her hands. It was still warm. Unsure what to do, she looked around but there was no one else in sight except the tramp.

"Excuse me," she said. "This bird is hurt."

The tramp looked up, slowly raising his eyes to her face. His head was made leonine by the mane of long greying hair and beard. She could smell him, now that she was close, but it strangely made him seem more human and less threatening. His face was crinkly brown and weather-beaten with eyes of indeterminate colour.

He grunted and held out one large hand. It had the same texture as his face and she felt its warmth as she slid the bird gently into his palm. He peered at it closely. He stroked the small body gently with a grimy finger and the bird stirred in his palm, the tiny beak opening and closing in distress.

He rose and carried it over to the water fountain, where he transferred a few drops of water with his finger to the chaffinch's beak. After a while it revived a little and seemed more aware. He murmured softly to it.

They returned to the bench and sat together watching the bird as it slowly recovered. After a few moments it suddenly took wing and flew off into the trees.

"Oh!" exclaimed Lucy smiling, "do you think it will be all right?"

The tramp grunted in response.

"Thanks," she said.

He waved her away.

"Actually I don't have to be home for hours yet," she said, trying to sound like a grown-up.

He wearily raised himself from the bench and strolled off down the path. She trailed along beside him.

"Where are you going? Do you have a home somewhere? Are you a real tramp?"

He paused, looked at her, but then carried on walking without answering. Lucy thought that it was a way of saying she had been impolite; maybe she had asked too many questions and she couldn't quite remember which order she had asked them. She tried to make amends.

"My name is Lucy. Are you hungry? I could get my mum to make you a sandwich."

He stopped again and waved her away.

"OK," said Lucy and she skipped off up the path. She had seen her brother and two of his cronies come in through the gate. She hoped they hadn't seen her.

"Hello," said Lucy. "I brought you that sandwich I promised you yesterday."

The tramp looked up and sighed but he managed a smile, and as he could see no one else in view, he accepted the sandwich.

He struggled over the dryness of the first bite.

"Peanut butter and strawberry jam. My favourite!" she said, sitting down beside him on the bench. "Where's your family now?"

He took another bite from the sandwich but made no reply.

Lucy brought him a sandwich most days but she often did not see him and if he could not be found in the park she would leave it for him wrapped in clingfilm. Sometimes she would find him still asleep in his place behind the public toilets cocooned in filthy blankets, newspapers and odd bits of cardboard.

More often than not he was surrounded by a few scattered bottles. Some were flat whiskey bottles that she recognised but there were many more of a larger greenish bottle with a crude label denoting a monk overshadowed by a stony monastery. She had no idea what they had once contained. Sometimes she picked up empties if he was not there and deposited them in the recycling bin.

He continued to ignore her, grunted occasionally if he had to and would roughly wave her away. He ate the sandwiches though.

"Hello," said Tim and kicked him in the face. He woke to darkness scattered by torchlight, confusion and pain. There were four or five of them surrounding him. They rained kicks and blows down on him with utter savagery while he, still tangled in his blankets and newspapers, could only curl into a ball and protect himself as best he could. They grew tired quickly; they were boys. One leant close to his face when the blows had seized.

"I'm Tim, and if I ever see you speak to my sister again I'll kill you." He spat into the tramp's face to seal his vow.

In the morning Tim woke Lucy with a pinch and told her that her tramp friend would never bother her again.

It was lunchtime by the time she had been allowed out to play. She made a sandwich and hurried over. She found him in his usual place still lying in his bedroll, his face puffy and blackened by dried blood. She fetched water for him in one of his empty bottles. He stirred as she dabbed his face with her dampened sleeve and sat up to drink some water.

"Should I get a doctor? Will I get my mum?" she asked, but he shook his head and signalled for her to help him up. She helped him to the door of the gents. He was inside a long time and when he came out he had cleaned himself and looked much better.

She helped him back to his bedroll. "Why do you stay here? Will you leave now?"

He sat on the ground, weary, exhausted, hopeless. Lucy felt more adult than ever before in her short life. She knelt beside him and put her arms around him. He pushed her away, grunted at her. She held his gaze calmly. She put her thin girlish arms around him again and pulled his head into her chest. She hugged him. She hugged him like only a child does.

"Mum, Mum, where's Tim?"

"He went to play baseball in the park, just a few minutes ago. Don't you go bothering him and his friends now."

Lucy's heart sank and she started pulling on her shoes as fast as she could.

Tim stood before him on the pathway; young, strong and arrogantly sixteen, and armed with a baseball bat. The tramp had been going somewhere. He worried now that he would be late. He looked at the boy and shook his head.

"You want me to throw the ball for you?"

Tim stepped menacingly forward, mouthing an obscenity.

Then he heard the car. They both heard it screech round the corner and accelerate down the long stretch towards the next corner and the gate.

He knew. He ran. He shed his long dirty coat, his jacket and his ragged cardigan as he gathered speed. He no longer needed anything, only to run.

Tim stared in amazement as the tramp sprinted past him heading for the gate. He turned and followed.

He ran, heart pounding, lungs straining, legs pumping, the blood surging through his veins. He ran. He broke sprint records that no-one would ever know or ever believe. They could not be repeated with a body that had to survive the event. He had no such restriction. His body was already burning all reserves of energy and oxygen. He heard the screech of brakes as the joyriders slowed for the second corner. He was too far away from the gate. He veered left, cutting across the grass and cleared the hedge and its protective fence in one leap. Tim, astounded, faltered and chose the gate.

He hit the pavement, running. Now his muscles were consuming their own tissue in their search for energy. No consequence, no protective functions, all survival instincts overridden. His joy was overwhelming; he knew his forgiveness, his fate. He heard the car revving through the gears, roaring up behind him. He saw Lucy racing out of her house and sprinting into the road. He sensed the car surging alongside. Lucy stopped dead in the middle of the

- 124 -

road transfixed by the scene - the man, head to head with the car bearing down on her, Tim a long way behind.

He leapt. His heart burst, flooding him with peace; he flew, no more effort now. The windscreen caught him and swallowed him up in a spray of glass. The car swerved and smashed into a lamp post; its front instantly sculpted into a perfect vee around it. The windscreen disgorged the body and it lay supported by the car, its back bent oddly around the post. Red blood ran off the top of the bonnet and mixed with the black oil gushing out from beneath. Stillness descended on the street.

Tim ran to Lucy. He swept her up into his arms. His chest aching for more air to speak with.

"How could he have known? I don't understand ... running so ....so fast....impossible... he saved you. We couldn't see, he couldn't have known."

Lucy saw much in her brother's eyes which she had never seen there before.

Diamond

The ladder seemed to stretch into infinity above him. He could not see the top. The reflected light from the yard below gave only a feeble glow up here. Paddy rested a moment, bringing his body in close to the rungs. He leaned his forehead against the cold steel and could feel through his skull the gentle thrum of the blast furnaces. He barely heard the harsh cacophony that was the continuous sound of the steelworks. It had been his working environment for close on fifteen years, but not like this, not like tonight. The cold wind fingered his hair and the collar of his jacket, making him feel exposed. He could not rest for long. He eased one shoulder and then the other trying to find a comfortable position for the dead weight tied on his back. The rain started again and he forced himself to move. He had climbed the hopper, where the scrap steel was stored, on many occasions and he knew it was only fifty feet or so, but tonight it seemed never ending. This time was different, each step, each handhold, each mark on the side of the giant bin must be discovered anew. His senses and his limbs must take each step as though for the first time, and like any first journey it seemed much longer.

He was close to the top now; he could see the rim. A little more effort and he was there, but not finished. He still had to mount the edge and then descend the ladder into the hopper itself and all the while the weight of his wife threatened to drag him down into the night.

He contemplated just letting go, now, letting their combined weight smash them on the concrete far below.

It would make fine gossip, but he could imagine how the stories would develop and where sympathy would lie. Bitch! Anger suddenly coursed through him replacing the insulating shock that had driven him this far. It gave him new strength as he made the dangerous transition from the outer ladder over the slippery lip of the hopper and onto the inner one. Inside it was warmer but much darker and he had no idea how full it was. He descended into the dark cautiously.

At last his feet found solidity. He kicked around and jumped once, all that his tired muscles would allow, to make sure the surface was stable. Finally he relaxed his grip on the ladder and leaning heavily against it, fumbled in the pocket of his donkey jacket for a knife and the small torch that he had brought with him. He sawed through the clothes line with difficulty and finally felt the body fall free. It was almost done. No more would she weigh him down. Paddy sank to his knees, while his spirits lifted with the absence of the burden from his shoulders. He needed to rest just for a little.

He hadn't planned it. It had happened two days ago, an accident really, one bloody row too many. He was almost sure he could have explained it away, but not sure enough. He had planned this though, to be rid of the body. He had drained the blood into the bath to make her lighter but that was all the touching he could manage. Afterwards, he had wrapped her in an old tartan rug and secured it with a clothes line until he decided what to do.

She had kept him in misery for too many years. He could not imagine how he had put up with it for so long; how he could have been seduced into marriage with her. He had feared her sharp tongue, she had scolded him incessantly often in public and in front of family and friends.

The final argument had been a repeat of many previous

ones. Taking advantage of an apparent rare good mood he had once again tentatively brought up the question of starting a family. She had always been dead set against the idea of having children. He had regretted his approach almost immediately as she had rapidly spiralled the fight into a shouting match beyond any reasonable hope of discussion - a common technique of hers. He was already backing down and trying to calm her when she had slapped him.

Only once before, had she slapped him, and then she had seen the look in his eyes and had known she had reached the limit, but it was not what she enjoyed anyway. She preferred more subtle methods. She was adept at lifting him with a few kind words and then savaging him mercilessly when his guard had dropped. She fed her enjoyment on the slow erosion of his self-esteem, sculpting him with her tongue and her disdain.

This time something deep inside him snapped and he hit her back – hard. Again and again and again.

He swept the small torch over the mass of discarded metal. He needed something to contain her, so she would not be seen as the scrap was transported to the furnaces and added to the melt for the next batch of steel.

Eventually, he doubled her over and forced most of her u-shaped body into a section of broken cast iron sewage pipe. He stood back, it was not entirely satisfactory but he had little to work with. Most of the scrap was too heavy to shift and moving around on the wet surfaces was hazardous.

One pale hand had broken loose from the rug. It was pushed out behind her. The torch caught the blue sparkle of the single diamond in her engagement ring. A ring she had insisted on and one far too big for his taste, or his hard earned cash come to that. It encircled the bright memories of an earlier time, of giving and choosing and sharing, but she had forfeited any right to fond memories; he wanted no reminders. He shoved the hand roughly back into its shroud. He used the rope to tie her in place and to secure the rug where it covered her outside the pipe.

It's done, he thought. I can do no more, now I leave it to fate. He looked up at the sky enclosed by the circular rim of the hopper. It was still dark and he could see a scattering of stars. He started the long climb upwards.

The Ocean Star had been smashing into heavy seas for several days now. Even her massive size and huge tonnage could not restrain the North Atlantic in winter. The waves, fat and heavy with no land to slow them, seemed intent on challenging her right to be there. Each signalled its displeasure by shouldering her aside.

Last night a flood alarm had sounded on the bridge. It indicated water in the fore-peak tank, the space immediately behind the bows and it most likely meant that there was some damage to the front of the ship. The old-man had taken five knots off, maintained their course and decided to wait until morning to investigate. Richard, as first officer, understood the need to keep schedules and please the company, but if he had been Captain he would have taken more drastic action. Still, it may be just a false alarm like the Captain hoped, and the old-man got paid to worry, the mate got paid to inspect the damage.

He checked the portable radio and the torch and nodded at the bosun who was sheltering from the spray under the lee of the fo'c's'le. He would stand watch at the hatch while Richard went down into the hold, and stay in contact with the radios.

The bosun assisted him over the coaming of the hatch

into the hold, while steadying himself with one hand against the constant rise and fall of the ship. Richard stood on a small platform just below the main deck. It was much warmer. The visual effect of the pitching was reduced, but the noise enhanced as the impact of each wave caused a sonic boom to reverberate through the hollow steel space. He directed the powerful beam from the torch onto the collision bulkhead that formed the front wall of the hold. It was the strongest bulkhead in the ship, designed to maintain the integrity of the hull in the event of a collision. In front of it was the fore-peak space and beyond that the hull narrowed to form the bows. From this vantage point he could clearly see the exposed skeleton of the ship. The struts and beams and ribs that supported the hull, like the inside of a whale only on a much larger scale.

It was a long trek down the access ladder to the bottom of the hold and then forward to the bulkhead and more inspection ladders to be climbed on that. He started the long descent. He stopped once half way down and keyed the send button twice on the radio; he was comforted by the repeat signal from the bosun who stood guard at the hatch. As Richard looked up he caught a glimpse of the bosun's arm silhouetted against the grey sky as he gave a reassuring wave.

He stood at the foot of the collision bulkhead, legs splayed against the movement, but his ears no longer registering the repeated boom of the waves. He laid the torch sideways on the bulkhead with the beam stretching diagonally upwards, laying a long line of light across the steel, like a rule. It was reassuring, the straightness of that line. Any deflection or bulge in the bulkhead would be easily seen. He moved the powerful lamp around in an arc trying other directions but the line of light stayed straight. As he moved the beam around a tiny spark of blue light flashed near the centre of the wall. The unlikely blueness of that spark caught his eye and he swept the area with the beam, but it did not re-occur.

He tested the open ended test valve, low down on the bulkhead and a stream of water shot out. That was no great surprise and it only let him know that there was some water in the bottom of the fore-peak tank. The next test valve was fifty feet above him.

He started up the inspection ladder bolted onto the collision bulkhead. At the next test valve he repeated the procedure, and again water issued. This was much more worrying as it meant that the fore-peak was flooded almost up to the waterline, so there was definitely a serious leak in the bow.

He radioed the bosun and brought him up to date. He asked him to relay the message to the bridge with the respectful suggestion to the Captain that a further reduction in speed was needed.

Richard liked the big ships, the supertankers. These were the largest moving structures ever built by man and he had sailed on the Ocean Star twice before. He laid the palm of his hand on the solid metal; it was alive with the vibration of the ship and the pulse of the sea. He slapped it affectionately - Clydebuilt, solid as a rock and built to last, holed or not in the bow. But, no matter how well built, he knew each year nature was reclaiming her, the corrosive soup of the sea and the always moist air dissolving a little more of the steel, gradually thinning her hull, returning her to the earth. The Star, even though she was many years younger than himself, would soon be due for the scrap yard, especially if she started costing the company money in repair bills. For now, they were empty of cargo and on their way to a refit in dry dock which should keep her going for several more years.

The pitching had become worse in the last few minutes and he held on to the handrail tightly as the ship lurched up and down. When it had eased a little, he commenced testing the top half of the bulkhead with the light beam. He was soon satisfied that all was well. As he lowered the lamp, he again saw the blue sparkle of light, much closer this time. He swept the beam around. There! A tiny shard of glass was embedded in the steel almost at the exact centre of the bulkhead. It seemed absurd. He rubbed his hand over the metal, flaking the rust away and it became a little clearer. It was so small he could barely see it. He brought his face up close. Now it clicked into focus and a smile broke on his face as he realised it was a perfectly faceted diamond embedded in the steel. It was starkly beautiful, its very smallness enhanced by the vast rusty plain in which it lay. He could not imagine how it came to be there.

He touched it with a fingertip and thought of possibilities. A diamond in the earth small enough to pass through all the processes that turn iron ore into steel, strong enough, even to survive the furnaces, and then entombed in the steel plate, but gradually over the years, working its way out with the flexing of the ship. Perhaps not so strange after all, he thought, pleased with his theory.

The diamond sat in a web of fine lines, exposed by his rubbing, as though someone had drawn a setting for it. His eyes were drawn to those lines and now he felt the smile slide from his face, felt the air seize in his throat and suddenly the noise of the sea smashed back into his senses. He realised that the diamond formed the hub of a web of cracks emanating in all directions. He pressed his hand against the bulkhead feeling the hard nub of the diamond dig into his palm. His hand came away damp. He tasted it with the tip of his tongue. Salt! Shit! He tasted again, not the insipid flatness of condensation but the rough flavour of the sea. Now seriously worried, he started quickly down the inspection ladder. He paused on the bottom plates to call the bosun on the radio and ordered him to relay his report on the condition of the collision bulkhead to the captain and the suggestion that they stop the ship to assess the damage more fully.

They should stop the ship. He doubted the integrity of the bulkhead. If it failed and her great engines continued to force her into the sea, then each bulkhead would collapse in turn, like dominoes, flooding the holds and the ship would drive itself downwards as it filled.

He started quickly up the access ladder, conscious now of each impact. The ladder seemed to stretch into infinity above him. The small circle of daylight beckoned him at the hatch. A thought occurred to him that the diamond had been faceted, worked on by man - his theory must be wrong.

The ship lurched as a particularly large wave hit them. He heard what he feared most, not the usual boom, but a grinding groan from the bulkhead and then much louder the low frequency scream of tearing metal muffled by the sea. Something worse had happen to the bow. He keyed the radio but there was no reassuring response. The ship still battered on into the swell; its engines relentlessly driving its massive bulk against the unyielding sea. The collision bulkhead must now take all the strain, but it was flawed, flawed by a perfect diamond. He hurried upwards. The ship must be stopped immediately.

On deck the bosun was in full flight back towards the superstructure, which housed the bridge, the accommodation and not least the lifeboats. It was still a quarter of a mile away. He had been sheltering in the fo'c's'le when he clearly heard what he guessed was a large section of the bow parting company from the ship. All his years at sea told him this was a good time to be the near the boats. He had passed on the earlier messages, but the ship had not yet slowed. The Captain had needed more convincing – too late, all the proof needed was on its way. He had the disconcerting feeling that the deck was sloping upwards, just slightly, it felt like he was beginning to run uphill and it was getting steeper all the time.

Richard kept climbing. Suddenly the bulkhead ruptured outward, the steel bent and twisted as easily as if it had been the petals of a flower. The colossal titanic roar of rushing water stilled his heart; and the hold began to rapidly fill below him, He climbed as fast as he could; he looked up, the steel rungs of the ladder stretched away forever. It was too far, but he kept climbing.

Paddy stood at the bedroom window sipping a mug of tea and looking out over the scar on the landscape that was only gradually healing. He had lived with this view for the last thirty years, ever since he had moved into this house with his new partner. The Ravenscraig steelworks had always dominated the town. The scrap steel hopper had long ago been removed as newer processes replaced the old but the faded blue corrugated tower that bore the works name in giant letters had only been demolished a few months ago and he still got a sense of something missing whenever he noticed the skyline.

Richard's mother had died almost a year ago. He was relieved when she finally gave up and let the cancer take her.

A large dark car turned into the street and drove slowly down the line of houses; too large and modern to belong to any of his neighbours he watched it for a moment and assumed it was lost. It pulled into the curb just outside his house.

He was just starting to get over her death and seeing his son again was going to help a lot. Richard's ship was due into Belfast for a refit in a few days and he had promised to spend some time at home.

The doorbell interrupted his thoughts. He set down his mug and with a last glance out of the window started for the stairs.

End.

19538881R00084

Printed in Great Britain
by Amazon